12-2017

First published in Great Britain in 2016 by Comma Press.
www.commapress.co.uk
Copyright © in the name of the individual contributor
This collection copyright © Comma Press 2016.

'Garments' by Tahmina Anam was first published in *Freeman's: Arrival* ©
Tahmima Anam 2016
'Morning, Noon & Night' by Claire-Louise Bennett was first published in
Pond © Claire-Louise Bennett 2016
'The Darkest Place in England' by Lavinia Greenlaw © Lavinia Greenlaw
2016
'In a Right State' by Hilary Mantel was first published in *The London
Review of Books* © Tertius Ltd. 2016.
'Disappearances' by K J Orr was first published in *Light Box* © K J Orr
2016.

This collection is entirely a work of fiction. The names, characters and
incidents portrayed in it are entirely the work of the authors' imagination.
Any resemblance to actual persons, living or dead, events, organisations or
localities, is entirely coincidental. The opinions of the authors are not
those of the publisher.

ISBN-13   978-1910974278
ISBN-10   1910974277

The publisher gratefully acknowledges the assistance of
Literature Northwest and Arts Council England across all its projects.

Set in Bembo 11/13 by David Eckersall.
Printed and bound by CPI Group (UK) Ltd, Croydon, CR0 4YY

THE BBC NATIONAL SHORT STORY AWARD

2016

WITH BookTrust

Contents

Introduction

AS A VORACIOUS READER for as long as I can remember – the newspaper at the age of two, a good book, hiding between the fire and the loaded clothes horse to avoid washday as a teenager, a bedtime devotee of a great novel for all my life – I was never a fan of the short story.

I often compared it to a takeaway meal – temporarily satisfying, but leaving you hungry soon after you've finished. For me the precious time available for reading was best served by a long and gripping narrative, with a beginning, a middle and end, that might keep me intrigued for days.

It may have been connected with my day job. Presenting a daily news or magazine programme on the radio is about rapid absorption of information, communicating ideas and stories in a few short minutes and, as one programme ends, preparation for the next one begins. Maybe my reading for pleasure and relaxation needed to take place over a more sustained period.

So, I accepted the request to chair the panel of judges for the 2016 BBC National Short Story

Award with BookTrust partly out of curiosity. What was it about the genre that so enthused so many of the literary friends for whom I had great respect?

Equally, would being required to read a carefully selected longlist culled from a vast range of authors – some established, some not – persuade me that the form could bring insight and delight in a completely different way from the longer work? I'm pleased and, frankly, relieved to report that it did.

From a long, long list of more than 400 entries, the panel of judges was each sent two large envelopes containing more than 60 manuscripts, ranging from 2000 to 8000 words in length. Every spare moment was spent reading and re-reading a quite spectacular variety of tales whose diverse subjects, styles and themes reveal the flexibility and confidence of short fiction now.

There were stories which drew on the lives of real people or fictional characters, ranging from William S. Burroughs, through Chekhov to Jane Eyre. There was comedy, tragedy and we were transported around the globe from Zimbabwe, into the Indian sub-continent, through South America and into the often dystopian future.

As readers we had no idea of the name of the author – we read everything blind initially – so we were basing our judgements purely on the quality of the prose and the narrative force of the story as we each selected our favourites.

There was a surprising amount of agreement

when we gathered to select the five stories that would constitute the final shortlist and appear in this book and on air. I'd heard there was often blood on the table when literary judging panels gathered to make their decisions. Despite an insightful debate, happily no violence ensued.

My panel contained the wonderful novelist, Pat Barker, Kei Miller, the poet, novelist and short story writer whose novel, *Augustown*, was published this summer to rave reviews, Ted Hodgkinson, senior programmer for Literature at the Southbank Centre and a long standing advocate of the short story and Di Speirs, the BBC's Books Editor, the driving force behind the prize, the woman responsible for keeping Radio Four at the forefront of the literary spoken word and a friend who's long endeavoured to persuade me of the joy of the genre.

We narrowed our final shortlist from unsettling stories set on beaches, in the undergrowth and against northern nights but in the end, the top five became very clear to us. Although they are diverse in style and subject they share certain underlying themes. A search for love, moments of connection, poised and perfect prose, and an understanding of the human condition.

The authors who made it to the shortlist are all professional writers – Hilary Mantel needs no introduction after a long career writing beautiful novels and finally hitting the big time with her Tudor series charting the life of Henry VIII's fixer, Thomas Cromwell.

Her story, 'In a Right State', will have echoes for anyone who's waited in the casualty department of a large NHS hospital and become aware that among the sick and sad are the homeless seeking warmth, sanctuary and company. It's written in Mantel's typically mordant style and grows funnier each time you read it. The characters leap from the page and draw you into the community of a small, but intriguing segment of society.

In 'Garments', Tahmima Anam takes us movingly into the lives of the women who earn a paltry living in a Bangladeshi sweat shop. Immediately you care about Jesmin who's 'six shirts behind' and laugh with her as she moves on to the panty order for the 'foreign ladies who use them to hold in their fat.' The women have strength even though they have no power and the story is told without a hint of sentimentality.

In 'Disappearances' by K J Orr, the guilt of the central character is heavy from the outset. We're in Buenos Aires in the company of a retired plastic surgeon as he reflects on the history of the country in which so many people suffered terribly, but in which he had an 'easy run through the years.' It's a simple and astute yet devastating tale.

'Morning, Noon and Night' by Claire-Louise Bennett is a slow burning story which portrays loneliness and the longing which comes as a result of unrequited love. It's witty in the most subtle way and the language is so beautiful I found myself reading it out loud over and over again for the sheer pleasure of speaking the words.

Lavinia Greenlaw's 'The Darkest Place in England' took me straight back to the day we moved to a remote part of the Peak District and found the lack of light pollution wonderful, but not for a teenage girl like Greenlaw's Jamie. She lies to her father and goes out with an unsuitable friend in a car full of boys. The writing is exceptional and the portrait of a young person taking stumbling steps towards adulthood is intensely moving.

So, I'm a convert. There's a compressed power in a great short story which draws you in, holds you tight and then echoes in your head for a very long time after.

Jenni Murray

Garments

Tahmima Anam

ONE DAY MALA LOWERS her mask and says to Jesmin, my boyfriend wants to marry you. Jesmin is six shirts behind so she doesn't look up. After the bell, Mala explains. For months now she's been telling the girls, ya, any day now me and Dulal are going to the Kazi. They don't believe her, they know her boyfriend works in an air-conditioned shop. No way he was going to marry a garments girl. Now she has a scheme and when Jesmin hears it, she thinks, it's not so bad.

Two days later Mala's sweating like it's July. He wants one more. Three wives. We have to find a girl. After the bell they look down the row of sewing machines and try to choose. Mala knows all the unmarried girls: which one needs a room, which one has hungry relatives, which one borrowed money against her wage and can't work enough overtime to pay it off. They squint down the line and consider Fatima, Keya, Komola, but for some reason or other they reject them all.

1

There's a new girl at the end of the row but when Mala takes a break and limps over to the toilet she comes back and says the girl has a milky eye.

There's a new order for panties. Jesmin picks up the sample. She's never seen a panty like it before. It's thick, with double seams on the front, back, and around the buttocks. The leg is just cut off without a stitch. Mala, she says, what's this? Mala says, the foreign ladies use them to hold in their fat and they call them Thanks. Thanks? Yep. Because they look so good, in the mirror they say to the panties, Thanks. Jesmin and Mala pull down their masks and trade a laugh when the morning supervisor, Jamal, isn't looking.

Jesmin decides it won't be so bad to share a husband. She doesn't have dreams of a love marriage, and if they have to divide the sex that's fine with her, and if he wants something, like he wants his rice the way his mother makes it, maybe one of them will know how to do it. Walking home as she did every evening with all the other factory workers, a line two girls thick and a mile long, snaking out of Tongi and all the way to Uttara, she spots a new girl. Sometimes Jesmin looks in front and behind her at that line, all the ribbons flapping and the song of sandals on the pavement, and she feels a swell in her chest. She catches up to the girl. Her name's Ruby. She's dark, but pretty. Small white teeth and filmy eyes. She's new and eager to make friends. I'm coming two, three hours from my village every morning, she complains. I know, Jesmin says. Finding a place to live is why I'm doing this.

The year Jesmin came to Dhaka she said to her father, ask Nasir-chacha to give you his daughter's mobile contact. Nasir-chacha's daughter Kulsum had a job in garments. Her father nodded, said, she will help you. Her mother, drying mustard in front of their hut, put her face in the crook of her arm. Go, go, she said. I don't want to see you again. Jesmin left without looking back, knowing that, once, her mother had another dream for her, that she would marry and be treated like a queen, that all the village would tell her what a good forehead she had. But that was before Amin, before the punishing hut.

Kulsum did help her. Put in a good word when she heard they were looking. She has a place, a room in Korail she shares with her kid and her in-laws. Her husband works in foreign so she lets Jesmin sleep on the floor. She takes half of Jesmin's pay every month. You're lucky, she tells her, I didn't ask for the money up front. But now her husband's coming back and Jesmin has to find somewhere else. She has another relative, a cousin's cousin, but he lives all the way out in Mogbajar and Jesmin doesn't like the way he looks at her. There's a shanty not far from the factory and she heard there were rooms going, but when she went to look, the landlord said, I can't have so many girls in my building. What building? Just a row of tin, paper between the walls, sharing an outside tap. But still he told her he wasn't sure, had to think about it. If you had a husband, he said, that would be a different story.

When Jesmin joined the line, she started as Mala's helper. She tied her knots and clipped the threads from her shirt buttons. The Rana strike was over and Mala's leg was broken and the bosses had their eye on her, always waiting to see if she'd make more trouble. Even now, Jamal gives her a look every time she walks by, waiting to see if she takes too long in the toilet. They would have got rid of her a long time ago if her hands weren't so good, always first in the line, seams straight as blades of grass, five, seven pieces ahead of everyone.

To make the Thanks you have to stretch the fabric tight against your left arm while running the stitch. Then you fold it, stretch again, run the stitch back up, till the whole thing is hard and tight. Jesmin trims the leg and takes a piece home. She pulls it up over her leg. Her thigh bulges in front and behind it. She doesn't understand. Maybe the legs of foreign ladies are different.

Jesmin and Mala know a foreign lady, Miss Bridgey. She came to the factory and asked them a few questions and wrote down what they said. How many minutes for lunch? Where is the toilet? If there's a fire, what will you do? In the morning before she came Jamal lined everyone up. There's an inspector coming, he said. You want to make a good impression. Jamal liked to ask a question and supply the answer. Are we proud of the factory? Yes we are! What do we think of Sunny Textiles? We love SunnyTex! That day they opened all the windows and did the fire drill ten times. Then Miss Bridgey showed up and Jesmin could see the laugh behind Jamal's face. He thought it would be a man in a suit, and there was this little yellow-haired girl. Nothing to worry. Aren't we lucky? Yes we are.

When Miss Bridgey comes back Jesmin is going to ask her about the Thanks. But right now they have to explain the whole thing to Ruby. Mala's doing all the talking. We marry him, and that way we can tell people we are married. We give him a place to stay, we give him food, we give him all the things a wife gives. If he wants sex we give him sex. When she mentions the sex Jesmin feels her legs filling up with water. Why don't we get our own husbands? Ruby asks. She's green, she doesn't know. Ruby looks like she's going to cry. Then she bites her full lip with a line of those perfect little teeth and she says, okay, I'll do it.

When Jesmin was born, her mother took a piece of coal and drew a big black mark behind her ear. Jesmin went to school and learned the letters and the sums before any of the other children. The teacher, Amin, always asked her to sing the national anthem on Victory Day and stand first in the parade. Amin said she should go to secondary. He said, meet me after school. He taught her sums and A, B, C. He put his hand over her hand on the chalk.

Miss Bridgey comes a few days later and she takes Jesmin aside. I'm worried about the factory, she says. Has it always been this bad? Jesmin looks around. She takes in the fans in the ceiling, bars on the windows, rows and rows of girls bent over their machines. It's the same, she says. Always like this.

This place good. This place okay. We love SunnyTex! But why, she asks Miss Bridgey, do the ladies in your country wear this? She holds up the Thanks. Miss Bridgey takes it from her hand, turns it around, then she laughs and laughs. Jesmin, you know how expensive these are?

On the wedding day Dulal comes to the factory. He's wearing a red shirt under the grey sleeveless sweater they made last year when the SunnyTex bosses decided to expand into knitwear. Jesmin and Mala and Ruby stand in front of him, and he looks at them with his head tilted to the side. Take a look at my prince! Mala says. He's got a narrow face and small black eyes and hair that sticks to his forehead. Now it's time to get married so they set off on two rickshaws, him and Mala in the front, Jesmin and Ruby following behind. They are all wearing red saris like brides do, except nobody's family has showed up to feed them sweets or paint their feet.

Jesmin watches the back of Mala and Dulal. She knows that Mala's brother died in Rana. That Mala had held up his photo for seven weeks, hoping he would come out from under the cement. That she was at the strike, shouting her brother's name. That her mother kept writing from the village asking for money, so Mala had to turn around and go back to the line. Mala's face was cracked, like a broken eggshell, until she found Dulal. Now she comes to the factory, works like magic, tells her jokes, does her overtime as if it never happened, but Jesmin knows that once you die like that, on the street or in the factory, your life isn't your life any more.

This morning Jesmin went to the shanty to talk to the landlord. I'm getting married. Can I stay? He looked at her with one side of his face. Married? Show me the groom. I'll bring him next week, she said. He took one more drag and threw his cigarette into the drain and Jesmin thought for sure he was going to say no, but then he turned to her and said, what, I don't get any sweets? Then he slapped her on the back, and she shrank, but it was a friendly slap, as if she was a man, or his daughter. Next she went to Kulsum. I found a husband. Good, she said, you're getting old. Now I don't have to worry about you.

Jesmin sees marriage as a remedy. If you are a girl you have many problems, but all of them can be fixed if you have a husband. In the factory, if Jamal puts you in ironing, which is the easiest job, or if he says, take a few extra minutes for lunch, you can finish after hours and get overtime, you can say, but my husband is waiting, and then you won't have to feel his breath like a spider on your shoulder later that night when the current goes out and you're still in the factory finishing up a sleeve. Everything is better if you're married. Jesmin is giving Ruby all this good advice as their rickshaw passes the Mohakhali flyover but the girl's eyes are somewhere else. Bet she had some other idea about her life. Jesmin puts her arm around Ruby's shoulder and notices she smells very nice, like the biscuit factory she passes on the way to SunnyTex.

Jesmin is the only one who can sign her name on the wedding register. The others dip their thumbs into ink and press them into the big book. The kazi takes their money and gives them a piece of paper that has all their names on it. Jesmin reads it out loud to the others.

After, Dulal wants to stop at a chotpoti stall. Three men, friends of his, are waiting there. They look at the brides, up and down, and then they stick their elbows into Dulal's side and Dulal smiles like he's just opened a drawerful of cash. Who's first? they ask him. The old one, he replies, not bothering to whisper it. Then that one, he says, pointing to Jesmin. Next week Kulsum said she would let Jesmin string a blanket across and take half the bed. Her in-laws will be on the other half and she'll take the kid and sleep on the floor. Best for last, eh? his friend says. Dulal looks at Ruby like he's seeing her for the first time and he says, yeah, she's the cream.

The friends take off and then it's just the brides and groom. They sit on four stools along the pavement. Jesmin feels the winter air on her neck. Where's your village? Dulal asks, but before she can tell him, she hears Ruby's voice saying, Kurigram. Something in the sound of her voice makes Jesmin think maybe Ruby wants to be the favourite wife. She notices now that Ruby has tied a ribbon in her hair. They finish their plates and Mala holds hands with Dulal and they take off in the direction of her place. Jesmin and Ruby are taking the bus to Kulsum's. Ruby's giving Kulsum some of her pay so she can stay there too, just until they find her somewhere else.

Jesmin wants to say something to mark the fact that they are all married now. She can't think of anything so she asks Ruby if it gets cold in her village. Yes, she says, in winter sometimes people die. I'm from the south, Jesmin tells her, it's not so bad but still in winter, it bites. They hug their arms now as the sun sets. I wonder what they're doing, Ruby says. Do you think he's nice? He looks nice.

They're doing what people do, she tells Ruby, at night when no one is looking. They arrive at Kulsum's. She can share your blanket, Kulsum says, throwing a look at Ruby until Ruby takes the money out of her bag. They warm some leftover rice on the stove Kulsum shares with two other families at the back of the building. The gas is low and it takes half an hour to heat the rice, then they crush a few chillies into it. I have three younger sisters, Ruby says, even though Jesmin hasn't asked about her family. Where are they? Home and hungry, she says, and Jesmin gets a picture in her mind of three dark-skinned girls with perfect teeth, shivering together in the northern cold. What about you? Ruby asks. A snake took my brother, Jesmin says, remembering his face, grey and swollen, before they threw it in the ground. Hai Allah! Ruby rubs her hand up and down Jesmin's back. His forehead was unlucky, Jesmin says, pretending it wasn't so bad, like this wasn't the reason everything started to go sour, her parents with nothing to look forward to, just a daughter whose head was a curse and the hope that next year's rice would come up without a fight.

It's freezing on the floor. Jesmin is glad for Ruby's back spreading the warm into their blanket. You are kind, Ruby mumbles as she falls asleep, and Jesmin can see her breathing, her shoulders moving up and down. She lies awake for a long time imagining Mala with their husband. The watery feeling returns to her legs. Ruby shifts, moves closer, and her biscuit smell clouds up around them. Jesmin takes a strand of Ruby's hair and puts it into her mouth.

When she gets to SunnyTex the next morning, Mala is already at her machine with her head down. Jesmin tries to catch her eye but she won't look up, and when they break for lunch she disappears and Jesmin doesn't see her until it's too late. Finally it's the end of the day and Mala is hurrying along in the going-home line. What d'you want? She squints as if she's looking from far away and when Jesmin asks her what the wedding night was like, she says, it wasn't so bad. That's all? You'll find out for yourself, don't let me go and spoil it, and then her face bends into a smile. She won't say anything else.

After their shift is over Jesmin tells Ruby, let's go to a shop. I don't have any money, Ruby says. Don't worry, we'll just look. They walk to the sandal shop at the end of the street. They stare at the wall of sandals. Ruby takes Jesmin's hand and squeezes her fingers. It's so nice she can almost feel the sandals on her feet.

The week is over and finally it's Jesmin's turn. She scrubs her face till Kulsum scolds her for taking too long at the tap. She wears a red shalwar kameez. Ruby wants to do her hair. She makes a braid that begins at the top of Jesmin's head and runs all the way down her back. Her fingers move quickly and Jesmin feels a shiver that starts at her neck and disappears into her kameez. Ruby reaches back and takes the clip out of her own hair and puts it into Jesmin's. She feels it tense her hair together.

All day while they're sewing buttons onto check shirts Jesmin can feel the clip pulling at her scalp. Mala, she says, I'm feeling scared. At first Mala looks like she's going to tell her something, but her eyes go back to her sewing machine and she says, all brides are scared. Don't worry, I tested him out for you. Equipment is working tip-top.

After work Dulal is standing outside the SunnyTex gate. He puts his finger under her chin and stares into her face like he's examining a leg of goat. His breathing is ragged and his cheeks are shining. She notices how dirty his shirt is under the sweater and she starts to wonder what sort of a man would want three wives all at once. She shakes her head to knock the thoughts out of it. She has a husband, that's what matters. The road unfolds in front of them as they walk home, his hand molded onto her waist.

Kulsum is wearing lipstick and she tells her kid, look, your khalu has come to visit, give him foot-salaam, and her kid kneels in front of Dulal and touches his sandal. In the kitchen they pass around

the food. Jesmin puts rice on Dulal's plate, and the
bigger piece of meat. Kulsum gets a piece too and
the rest of them do with gravy. She's given him the
mora from under the bed so he sits taller than
everyone else. The gravy is watery but Jesmin
watches Kulsum's kid run his tongue all across his
plate. She thinks about Ruby. It's Thursday and she's
gone home on the bus to spend the weekend with
her brothers. Jesmin fingers the clip, still standing
stiff on the side of her head.

Now it's time and they lie down together. The
blanket is strung across but Jesmin can see the
outline of Kulsum's mother-in-law, her elbow
jutting into their side of the bed. Dulal turns his face
to the wall and says, scratch my back. He squirms
out of his shirt and she runs her fingers up and
down his back and soon her nails are clogged with
dirt. He takes her hand and pulls it over to the front
of his body, and then he takes out his thing. His
hand is over her hand, and she thinks of Amin and
the chalk and the village, fog in the winter and the
new season's molasses and everything smelling clean,
the dung drying against the walls of her father's hut.
Her arm is getting sore and Dulal's breath is slow
and steady, his thing soft as a mouse. She thinks
maybe he's fallen asleep but then he turns around
and she feels the weight of him pressing down on
her. He drags down her kameez and tries to push
the mouse in. After a few minutes he gives up and
turns back around. Scratch my back, he says,
irritated, and finally he falls asleep with her hand
trapped under his elbow.

The next day is Friday and Dulal says he's going to spend it with his sister, who lives in Uttara. Jesmin was hoping they could go to the market and look at the shops, but he leaves before she can ask. She takes the bus to Mohakhali. Mala's neighbour looks Jesmin up and down and says to her, so your friend is married now. Look at her, like a queen she is. Mala's wearing bright orange lipstick and acting like something good has happened to her. She's talking on her mobile and Jesmin waits for her to finish. Then she asks, is it supposed to be like that?

Mala looks up from the bed. You couldn't do it?

What, what was I supposed to do?

She grabs an arm. Did he put it in?

No.

She curses under her breath. But I told him you would be the one.

The one to what?

The one to cure his, you know, not being able to.

Jesmin struggles to understand. You told me his equipment was tip-top.

Mala shrinks from her. It occurs to Jesmin that she never asked the right question, the one that has been on everyone's mind. Why does a guy working in a shop, who doesn't get his hands dirty all day, want a garments girl, especially a broken one like Mala? Jesmin stares at her until Mala can't hold her eye any more. Mala looks down at her hands. I paid him, she says.

You paid him?

Then he started asking for more, more money, and I didn't have it, so I told him you and Ruby would fix him. That's the only way he would stay.

She's got her head in her hands and she's crying. She rubs her broken leg, and Jesmin thinks of Rana, and Mala's brother, and her own brother, and she decides there's nothing to be done now but try and fix Dulal's problem, because now that they were married to him, his bad was their bad.

What next?

Try again, try everything. Mala hands her the tube of lipstick. Here, take this.

That night Jesmin asks Kulsum for a few sprays from the bottle of scent she keeps in a box under the bed and Kulsum takes it out reluctantly, eyeing her while she pats some of it onto her neck. Jesmin draws thick lines across her eyelids and smears the lipstick on hard. Dulal cleans his plate and goes outside to gargle into the drain. She stands with him at the edge of the drain and after he rinses and spits he looks up at the night. There's all kinds of noise coming from the compound, kids screaming, dogs, a radio, but up there it looks quiet. Maybe Dulal's looking for a bit of quiet, too. Fog's coming, she says. She asks about his sister. Alhamdulillah, he tells her, but doesn't say, I will take you to meet her. I hate winter, he says instead, makes my bones tired.

Winter makes her think of the sesame her mother had planted, years ago when she was a baby. The harvest was for selling, but after the first season the price at the market wasn't worth the water and the effort, so she gave it up. But still the branches came up, twisted and pointy every year, tearing the feet off anyone who dared walk across the field. Only Amin knew how to tread between the bushes, his feet unscarred, the soles of his feet always so soft. Jesmin ran them across her cheeks and it was like his palm was touching her, or the tip of his penis, rather than the underside of his big toe, that's how delicate his feet were. I'm only here to talk, he said, telling her the story of Laila and Majnu. From Amin she learned what it was to be swallowed by a man, like a snake swallowing a rat, whole and without effort. He pressed his feet against her face, showing her the difference between a schoolteacher and a farmer's daughter, and she licked the salt between his toes, and when she asked when they would get married, he laughed as if she had told him the funniest joke in the world. And then his wife went to the Salish, and the Salish decided she had tempted Amin, and they said, leave the village. But not before you are punished. And into the punishing hut she went, and when she came out, she looked exactly like she was meant to look, ugly and broken. Like a rat swallowed by a snake. Just like Mala looked after they told her the search was over and she would never see her brother again. Now Jesmin is wondering if something happened to Dulal that made him feel like the rest of them, like a small animal in a big, spiteful world.

Maybe that's why, she offers, speaking softly into the dark. He turns to her. What did you say?

Maybe that's why, you know, it's not – it's not your fault.

He comes close. His breath is eggy. That's when, out of nowhere, one side of her face explodes. When she opens her eyes she's on the ground and everyone is standing over her, Kulsum, her kid, her in-laws, and Dulal. The kid tugs at her kameez and she stands up, brushes herself off. No one says anything. Jesmin can taste lipstick and blood where she's bitten herself.

In the morning Jamal takes one look at her and runs her to the back of the line. You look like a bat, he says, you should've stayed home. What if that inspector comes nosing around? Her eye is swollen so she has to change the thread on the machine with her head tilted to one side. Ruby's back from her village and when she sees Jesmin she starts to cry. Don't worry, Jesmin says, it's nothing. She takes a toilet break, borrows a compact from Mala and looks at herself. One side of her face is swallowing the other. When she comes out Ruby's holding a choc bar. She presses it against Jesmin's cheek and they wait for it to melt, then they tear open a corner and take turns pouring the ice cream into their mouths.

They go home. Dulal isn't there. Now look what you did, Kulsum says. They wait until the mosquitoes come in and finally everyone eats. When the kerosene lamp comes on and she's about to bed on the floor with Ruby, Dulal bursts in and demands food. She makes him a plate and watches him belch. The food's cold, he says. After, it's the same, lying there facing his back, holding his small, lifeless thing, except this time Ruby's on the floor next to Kulsum and her kid. Scratch my head, Dulal mutters. He falls asleep, and later, in the night, she hears him cry out, a sharp, bleating sound. She thinks she must have dreamt it because in the moonlight his face is as mean as ever.

On the day of Ruby's turn, she looks so small. When she's cut too much thread off her machine, Jamal scolds her and she spends the rest of the day with her head down. But after lunch she goes into the toilet and when she comes out she's got a new sari on and the ribbon is twisted into her hair like a thread of happy running all around the back of her head. Dulal comes to the gate and when he sees Ruby his face is as bright as money. Ruby says something to Dulal and he laughs. Jesmin watches them leave together, holding hands, her heart breaking against her ribs. Jesmin covers her ears against the sound of laughter. In the punishing hut, the Salish gathered. The oldest one said, take off your dress. When her clothes were on the ground he said, walk. They sat in a circle and threw words like rotten fruit. She's nothing but a piece of trash. Amin said: her pussy stinks like a dead eel. She is the child of pigs. She's a slut. She's the shit of pigs. Walk, walk. Move your hands. You want to cover it now? Where was your shame when you seduced a married man? Get out now. Get out and don't come back. Afterward, they laughed.

Jesmin covers her ears against the sound of laughter.

It's Friday. She packs her things and says goodbye to Kulsum. The kid wraps his legs around her waist and bites into her shoulder. She hands money to the landlord and he waves her to the room. There's a kerosene lamp in one corner, and a cot pushed up against another. Last year's calendar is tacked to the wall. The roof is leaking and there's a large puddle on the floor. She sees her face in the pool of water. She sees her eyes and the shape of her head and Ruby's clip in her hair. She opens her trunk and finds the pair of Thanks she stole from the factory. She holds it up. It makes the silhouette of a piece of woman. She pulls the door shut and the room darkens. She takes off her sandals, her shalwar. She lies on the floor, the damp and the dirt under her back, and drags the Thanks over her legs. When she stands up she straddles the pool of water and casts her eyes over her reflection. There is a body encased, legs and hips and buttocks. The body is hers but it is far away, unreachable. She looks at herself and hears the sound of laughter, but this time it is not the laughter of the Salish, but the laughter of the piece of herself that is closed. She knows now that Ruby will fix Dulal, that she will parade with him in the factory, spreading her small-toothed smile among the spools of thread that hang above their heads, and that Dulal will take Ruby to his air-conditioned shop, and her sisters will no longer be hungry, and Jesmin will be here, joined by the laughter of her own legs, no longer the girl of the punishing hut, but a garments girl with a room and a closed-up body that belongs only to herself.

The door opens. Jesmin turns to the smell of biscuits.

Morning, Noon & Night

Claire-Louise Bennett

SOMETIMES A BANANA WITH coffee is nice. It ought not to be too ripe – in fact there should be a definite remainder of green along the stalk, and if there isn't, forget about it. Though admittedly that is easier said than done. Apples can be forgotten about, but not bananas, not really. They don't in fact take at all well to being forgotten about. They wizen and stink of putrid and go almost black.

Oatcakes along with it can be nice, the rough sort. The rough sort of oatcake goes especially well with a banana by the way – by the way, the banana might be chilled slightly. This can occur in the fridge overnight of course, depending on how prescient and steadfast one is about one's morning victuals, or, it might be, and this in fact is much more preferable, there's a nice cool windowsill where a bowl especially for fruit can always be placed.

A splendid deep wide sill with no wooden overlay, just the plastered stone, nice and chilly: the perfect place for a bowl. Even a few actually, a few bowls in fact. The sill's that big it can accommodate three sizeable bowls very well without appearing the least bit encumbered. It's quite pleasant, then, to unpack the pannier bags and arrange everything intently in the bowls upon the sill. Aubergine, squash, asparagus and small vine tomatoes look terribly swish together and it's no surprise at all that anyone would experience a sudden urge at any time during the day to sit down at once and attempt with a palette and brush to convey the exotic patina of such an irrepressible gathering of illustrious vegetables, there on the nice cool windowsill.

Pears don't mix well. Pears should always be small and organised nose to tail in a bowl of their very own and perhaps very occasionally introduced to a stem of the freshest redcurrants, which ought not to be hoisted like a mantle across the freckled belly of the topmost pear, but strewn a little further down so that some of the scarlet berries loll and bask between the slowly shifting gaps.

Bananas and oatcakes are by the way a very satisfactory substitute for those mornings when the time for porridge has quite suddenly passed. If a neighbour has been overheard or the towels folded the day's too far in and porridge, at this point, will feel vertical and oppressive, like a gloomy repast from the underworld. As such, in all likelihood, a submerged stump of resentment will begin to perk up right at the first mouthful and will very likely preside dumbly over the entire day. Until, finally, at around four o'clock, it becomes unfairly but inevitably linked to someone close by, to a particular facet of their behaviour in fact, a perpetually irksome facet that can be readily isolated and enlarged and thereupon pinpointed as the prime cause of this most foreboding sense of resentment, which has been on the rise, inexplicably, all day, since that first mouthful of porridge.

Some sort of black jam in the middle of porridge is very nice, very striking in fact. And then a few flaked almonds. Be careful though, be very careful with flaked almonds; they are not at all suitable for morose or fainthearted types and shouldn't be flung about like confetti because almonds are not in the least like confetti. On the contrary, flaked almonds ought not to touch one another and should be organised in simple patterns, as on the side of a pavlova, and then they are quite pretty and perfectly innocuous. But shake out a palmful of flaked almonds and you'll see they closely resemble fingernails that have come away from a hand which has just seen the light of day.

Black jam and blanched fingernails, slowly sinking into the oozing burgoo! Lately, in the mornings, Ravel, played several times over, has been a very nice accompaniment indeed. And this, for now, is how, with minor variations, the day begins.

My own nails are doing very well as a matter of fact, indeed, I'm not sure they have ever done better. If you must know I painted them in the kitchen last Wednesday after lunch, and the shade I painted them right there in the kitchen is called Highland Mist. Which is a very good name, a very apt name, as it turns out. Because, you see, the natural colour of my nail, both the white part and the pink part, is still just about visible beneath the polish, it hasn't been completely obscured. And as time passes the polish doesn't chip away as such, it just sort of thins out around the edges, so now, as well as being able to see the white part and the pink part, the soot beneath the tips is also clearly visible. There, through the mist, which is of course the colour of heather, I can see coal dust beneath my fingernails. When the nails aren't painted at all this dirt has no other effect besides looking grubby and unkempt, but under the thinning sheen of Highland Mist something further occurs to me when I consider my hands. They look like the hands of someone very charming and refined who has had to dig themselves up out of some dank and wretched spot they really shouldn't have fallen into. And that amuses me, that really amuses me.

Indeed, it wouldn't be entirely unwarranted to suggest that I might, overall, have the appearance and occasionally emanate the demeanour of someone who grows things. That's to say, I might, from time to time, be considered earthy in its most narrow application. However, truth is, I have propagated very little and possess only a polite curiosity for horticultural endeavours. It's quite true that bright green parsley grows out of a pot near my door but I did not grow it from seed, not at all – I simply bought it already sprouted from a nearby supermarket, turned the plant out its plastic carton and shoved its compacted network of roots and soil here, into the pot next to my door.

Prior to that, some years ago, when I lived near the canal, I could plainly see from my bedroom window a most idyllic piece of land, encircled by the gardens of houses in back-to-back streets which thereby rendered it landlocked and enticing. It seemed impossible to get to the garden yet when I tore after a cat early one day he led me directly to it, whereupon he skedaddled sharpish and left me a tortured wren to cradle and fold. The wren had sung above my head for many weeks in the sunshine while I wrote letters in the morning and so it was only natural for me to cry out when I found it maimed and silent on the moss beneath the privet hedge. I was so upset I wanted to take that cat to a hot pan and sear its foul backside in an explosion of oil. I'll make you hiss you little shit. Never mind. I was in the garden that nobody owned or imposed upon and now that I had come here once I could come here again, surely. That's how it worked when I was a child anyhow, and I don't suppose these matters change a great deal.

I made sly enquiries just as a child does but unfortunately in contrast to a child I was listened to rather too attentively and so I quickly devised a wholesome reason for wishing to know who owned the land and whether I might visit it from time to time. It would be a very excellent place to grow things I'm sure I said and despite having never demonstrated any enthusiasm for gardening before and despite my statement of interest being really rather vague my proposition was taken seriously and since it turned out the land was in fact owned by the Catholic Church I was directed to the large house on the corner where the parish priest himself resided. This development was not something I had foreseen, truth be told I'd had no purposeful intentions. I think I just fancied the idea of having a secluded place to stand about in now and then, a secret garden if you like. And I should never have said a word about it because as usual the minute I did it all became quite misshapen and not what I had in mind at all, and yet there was something so alien and absurd about how it was all progressing that I couldn't help but go right along with it.

He was pleasantly perfunctory and did not mention anything at all about God, though he did enunciate the word bounty rather pointedly, but I didn't flinch. Where do you live? he said. Over in that house there, I said, and pointed through the window at a house across the road. He didn't look in the direction of my finger, it was quite sufficient for him that I could stand where I was and at the same time point to my house, and so it was settled. I do not remember the interior of the priest's house. I think the wallpaper in the hallway might have been sage green. It could be the case that I went in no further than the hallway. Perhaps I just stood at the door on the street looking in at the hallway. And then down at the plastic step. Yes, I believe he was wearing trainers in fact.

Clearing a decent area of ground and making it ready for planting potatoes was hard and monotonous work added to which early spring tends to be rather humid here and indeed it was so that particular year. I do not know fully what drove me to deracinate thick and fuzzy weeds like that every day in the premature heat. I often stopped and stood quite still, wondering what hopes my mind had just then been taken up with, but I could seldom recall. However, in spite of my own bemusement, for the first time in my adult life other people knew exactly what I was doing. It was as plain as day to them. I'd come back with the tools and lean them against the house wall and go inside to wash my hands and it would be quite clear to anyone who saw me what I had been doing that day. I believe during that period people were, notwithstanding two or three specific incidents, conspicuously more agreeable towards me.

As with most mensurable areas of life I demonstrated no ambition whatsoever as a grower and selected to cultivate low-maintenance crops only. Potatoes, spinach, and broad beans. That was it. That was enough. People told me what a cinch it was to grow courgettes, squash, marrow, carrots, but nothing had changed really – I hadn't suddenly become a gardener, and I resented being spoken to as though I had. The plants were coming on quite nicely when I received an invitation to speak at a very eminent university across the water upon a subject I was very interested in indeed – though not necessarily in a meritorious way. That's to say my interest was far too personal and not strictly academic and so my methodology came across as nostalgic and my perspective rather naive since I ignored the usual critical frameworks which were anyhow quite incomprehensible to me and instead pilfered haphazardly from the entire history of Western literature in order to strengthen my argument, which I cannot now recall. It had something to do with love. About the essential brutality of love. About those adventitious souls who deliberately seek out love as a prime agent of total self-immolation. Yes, that's right. It attempted to show that in the whole history of literature love is quite routinely depicted as an engulfing process of ecstatic suffering which finally, mercifully, obliterates us and delivers us to oblivion. Dismembered and packed off. Something like that. Something along those lines. I am mad about you. I am going out of my mind. My soul burns for you. I am inflamed. There is nothing now, nothing except you. Gone, quite gone. That kind of thing. I don't think it went down very well.

In fact I think it was considered rather unsophisticated and I remember feeling, despite my new floral chemise, suddenly sullen and practically Gothic. Actually, now that I come to think of it, I think the gist of my argument was simply that love is indeed a vicious and divine disintegration of selfhood and that artistic representations of it as such aren't at all uncommon or outlandish and have nothing whatsoever to do with endeavouring to shock an audience. There was an awful lot of violence you see in the work of the playwright the conference was reputedly reassessing and by and large that violence had hitherto been widely interpreted as nothing more than a dramatic strategy designed to shock, which I could never quite accept because how on earth is there anything shocking about violence? Anyway, I must confess, in order to establish a perennial language of love that testified to the abominable emancipation that is brought on by want of another I did in fact reference not only Sappho, Seneca, Novalis, Roland Barthes, Denis de Rougemont and Dutch historian Johan Huizinga I also included lyrics by PJ Harvey and Nick Cave, with the somewhat misplaced intention of demonstrating that it just never stops. That the desire to come apart irrevocably will always be as strong, if not stronger, than the drive to establish oneself. *As deep as ink and black, black as the deepest sea.*

Afterwards, when people were milling about and nodding in little groups, and I wasn't sure which of the several exits to make immediate use of, one of the academic big guns approached me and commented upon my paper. This all happened several years ago by the way – and I'm not absolutely sure why I'm recounting it here since it hardly situates me in a very flattering light – anyway, I don't recall exactly what he said to me, but it was exceedingly condescending and I very very clearly remember thinking why don't you fall over. Why don't you become tangled in some cables near the screen at the front on your way out and fall over and why don't you smack your head off a very sharp corner of the desk where earlier I sat and delivered my oh so charming missive and cut your head open ever so slightly so that a little bit of blood drops out. Just a little trickle of blood so that you don't look injured, only stupid and a bit iffy. Thank you very much, I said. And suddenly my back went cold so I deduced that the outside must after all be right there behind me; I turned around and walked towards it and very soon the ground did in fact change. It was wet and the car park was almost empty and smelt exclusively of dishcloths.

I may as well mention that I was staying with a girl I'd met in London the previous year. She was a very gifted academic and her ability to formulate a rousing opinion in response to something that had just happened or had just been said never ceased to impress and baffle me. How anyone could sally forth thoughts that were unfailingly well-formed and *de rigueur*, so soon and in any situation, was quite beyond me. She lived in a terrace house with several other postgraduate students, one of whom was a bloke as a matter of fact, and later, when my friend had gone to bed, he came into the sitting room where I sat with a large book flopped in my lap and put a hot water bottle underneath my toes. We didn't kiss then; we kissed later, a few weeks later. I flew home first and then we wrote to each other and then we really needed to see each other. So I went back, and then we kissed.

None of that has anything to do with now by the way. Despite how promising I seem to have made the encounter with the man and the hot water bottle sound it was in fact an ill-starred liaison and, perhaps less surprisingly, the inviability of my academic career eventually acquired a palpability of such insidious force that one day I came out of a shop unwrapping a pack of cigarettes and went nowhere for approximately half an hour. My wherewithal had quite dried up you see, I'd snubbed it for so long it had completely dried up and so I had come to a standstill, not knowing at all whether to turn left or go right. And the chief reason why I moved after approximately half an hour is because people continually approached me to enquire if the bus had already come and gone. 'I don't know', I said. 'I don't know,' I said again. 'I don't know.' And then it was as though they backed away and vanished completely and I was left standing absolutely and purposelessly alone – I don't think I've experienced a sense of fundamental redundancy to that extent since. The hopelessness of everything I was trying to occupy myself with was at last glaringly crystal clear.

But the potato plants were still growing! I went over to see my upbeat boyfriend many times and the potatoes and spinach and broad beans didn't mind one bit and sometimes while I was away I would lie in bed next to him unable to sleep and think of the potatoes and spinach and broad beans out there in the dark and I'd splay my fingers towards the ceiling and feel such yearning! I could recall the soil very well, how dark it was and the smell of it – as if it had never before been opened up, and the canal was nearby, and the moon was always overhead, and spiders would get off their webs for a bit and tentatively come into contact with the still edges of things. We didn't get along very well but this had no bearing whatsoever on our sexual rapport which was impervious and persuasive and made every other dwindling aspect of our relationship quite irrelevant for some time. We wrote each other hundreds of lustful emails, and by that I mean graphic and obscene. It was wonderful. I'd never done that before, I'd never written anything salacious before, it was completely new to me and I must say I got the hang of it really very quickly. I wish I'd kept them, I wish I hadn't become quite so unhinged when finally we acknowledged that eighteen months was pretty well as much as we could expect from a relationship based almost entirely upon avid fornication, and thereupon rashly expunged our complete correspondence, which, by then, amounted to almost two thousand emails. I won't be able to write emails like that again you see – that's to say I won't be able to write emails like that for the first time again. And that really was what made them so exciting – using language in a way I'd not used it before, to transcribe such an intimate area of my being that I'd never before attempted to linguistically lay bare. It was very nice I must say to every now and then take a break from cobbling together yet another overwrought academic abstract on more or less the same theme in order to set down, so precisely, how and where I'd like my brains to be fucked right out.

It wasn't all one way of course. He came to see me, and in fact he ate some of the vegetables I'd grown and he said they were lovely, which they were. We ate oranges too, quite often – in fact eating Spanish oranges became a bit of a thing. They are very nice to eat, oranges, when you've been having sex for ages. They cut through the fug and smell very organised, and so a sort of structure resumes and then it is perfectly possible to make a plan, such as going out somewhere nice for dinner.

Still, as I've said, none of this has anything to do with now whatsoever. I don't know what it has to do with and as a matter of fact I'm not sure what now is about either. I can say that I'm waiting for the delivery of two Japanese tapestries I bought in France earlier this year, but even that is off-the-mark and could very well proffer a misleading impression of me, a rather grand impression perhaps, as if I were supremely but subtly well-off and presided over quite the sequestered emporium of exotic whatnots and *recherché objets d'art*. Castles in the clouds I'm afraid, truth is, they can hardly be thought of as tapestries at all – they aren't much more than two pieces of old black cloth in two separate frames with some rose-gold flecks here and there, amounting, in one, to a pair of hands, and to a rather forlorn profile in the other. From what I remember of them it seems there had originally been many more stitches and thus a more complete and detailed image but for a reason I cannot at all decipher most of the stitches have been removed. Yet the trace of where they once

were is discernible with some effort, as of course
are the very small holes, where silken thread,
presumably, moved deftly in and out of the cloth. I
should think that in here especially they will only
ever look like two framed fragments of black cloth.
That's if they ever arrive of course – the man
bringing them over was due at seven o'clock and
it is now gone half past.

After that I lived in a shared house with my
very own bathroom. Not an en suite by the way. I
don't see what all the fuss is about where en suites
are concerned. In my opinion they're nearly always
rather dreary, and as a rule I think it's much nicer
to leave a room entirely before entering another.
Added to which I couldn't stand being naked in
my bedroom, even the thought of being naked in
sight of my bedroom was quite awful, yet at the
same time I couldn't stand being dressed either –
dressing myself made me cringe, it felt pathetic and
irrelevant, and of course I never stopped knowing
that the fingers pushing the buttons up through
the holes would be the same fingers that would
later push them back out again. Increasingly, very
long baths down the hall became my only respite
– I'm really not sure what would have happened at
all had the two rooms been adjoined. In the end I
spent too long in there. Hours and hours in fact. I
didn't know where else to go you see. I'd sit at my
desk from time to time, but that was all over with.
That's right, I'd thrown in the towel at last. It
hadn't worked out. I stopped doing what I wasn't
really doing and got a job in a bicycle repair shop

which turned out to be quite fortuitous because very soon after I began working there I urgently needed a new bike. I had a bike but I needed a new one, a different one, one with gears, one that could go up hills, one that could go up hills and carry shopping, one that felt sturdy and safe at night along roads where there is no light, one that could go up hills.

I saw it first through the hedgerow. It was summer and the hedgerow was very thick and actually almost impossible to see through but if you parted the leaves carefully, just a little bit, you could see all the way through − but you had to be careful, because of the bright flowers that extended, like dancers on tiptoes, everywhere among the hedgerow's branches. That can't be it, I said to my friend. Do you think that's it? I stepped back and stood in the road and looked downhill then uphill. It must be it, I said. There's nothing else. It's perfect, she said. I can't believe it, I said. Then we both peered through the hedge silently and I knew that of course this was it.

Placemats aren't really my thing to be perfectly honest but it looks as if I'm going to have to buy some to put beneath the bowls on the windowsill. Evidently the stone there has become rather too cold and possibly a bit damp because the other day an orange went off very quickly and I see today that the aubergine has developed some moist fluff in the shape and hue of an oyster. I ought to go down to the compost bin, it seems I have been putting it off.

I think I've lost interest in it actually, it's got very boring. Someone told me the other day that they had worms escaping from theirs, which I thought sounded quite momentous. I like worms and have no problem picking them up, which is unusual and thus gives me a clear advantage in certain situations because it means I can fling them at people if I feel like it and that never fails to cheer me up. There's a blue plastic bowl in the kitchen on the worktop where I collect scraps and skins and teabags and rinds and stalks and weeping leaves and shells etc for the compost bin and the idea was to use a smallish bowl so that I would empty it often, daily in fact, but I don't do that. I don't do that and it piles up, it all piles up and sometimes, though this happens rarely, I tip it all into a bigger bowl and just carry on.

Carry on with what? Well, for your information, there are always things that must be done – this, for one thing, after the fire has been lit of course. The birds need feeding at least once a day this time of year. And after a while I make the bed. I go up the steps and take a look in the post box. I like a coffee first thing. Sometimes I have a banana along with it. Sometimes that's all I need. And the blue bowl gets emptied, or not, into the compost bin. And the enamel bucket taken without fail to the side of the cottage and filled up with coal again and again. And because there is no step everything gets in here so there is never a time when the floor couldn't do with a good sweep. And of course there is always something to fold.

I texted the man, whose estranged wife is a

very dear friend of mine, and asked him if he'd
fallen asleep – I really couldn't think what else
might have happened to him. He texted back right
away to say he was en route. He brought a bag of
wood with him that had come from trees in his
own garden and a bottle of wine that came from
the country where his estranged wife – my dear
friend – now lives. It was a wine I was familiar
with and it was jarring, sort of, to drink it here, at
this time, without her. The Japanese frames and
their pared back interiors were in a large cotton
bag which he leant against the ottoman beneath
the mirror. I did not go near the bag and perhaps
he supposed I had no real interest in the contents
but I didn't want to look at the pieces in front of
him, I wanted to be alone, because in that way I
wouldn't have to come up with something to say
about them. In circumstances when an impression
is extended for the benefit of the person looming
nearby whatever is said is rarely anything at all
evocative and the moment it is said something
intrinsic is circumvented and cannot be recaptured
later on. Anyhow, I didn't mind waiting – waiting
was a pleasure in fact. Anticipation, when it occurs,
often makes me animated and expansive, as if I am
perhaps reviving and honing my senses in
preparation for the awaited object: yes indeed, the
world is a scintillant and fascinating place when a
half-remembered mystery leans within reach. He
stayed for an hour and we talked about the three
sons and renting apartments abroad and the recent
success of a mutual friend and now and then he

expressed deliberately autocratic views in order to rile me but in fact he was wasting his time because I could not be offended – on the contrary, I found a great deal to be amused by, and it might be that my irreverent attitude threw him; some people would much rather make you cross it seems. We may have mentioned Christmas, I do not recall. Even after he left I did not go to the bag directly – I took his emptied glass and the wine cooler out to the kitchen, I arranged the wood he'd kindly given me, I hung up a coat – the wine you see had gone gallivanting through my blood and I didn't want to come at the pictures with a giddy head full of fanciful expectation. So I waited a while longer, until a more subdued atmosphere was restored, and then I went to the bag and lifted out the heavy frames; focused and unfazed – like a connoisseur.

There are six and a half small flowers. Their petals are small and heart-shaped. Scattered about them are individual petals, these are not heart-shaped and they are slightly darker, as if falling further away. A pair of hands reaches up to the flowers, just the outline of a pair of hands and the edge of one sleeve of a kimono. There is a face, turned, not looking up towards the hands, not at all concerned with the hands' activity: the forehead, the heavy eyelids, the pursed lips, and an earring. All of this occurs in just one small diagonal area of the cloth, the rest is in blackness. And it is the same face in the second frame, where there are even fewer stitches. And while I look at this downcast profile and the few vertical lines which denote, again, the fabric of a heavy kimono, I realise I was quite wrong. Nothing had been undone; there hasn't ever been more than this. What I saw, what I can still see when I stand close enough, was the idea – the plan – of course! Whoever created these did not remove stitches with the intention, as I had initially suspected, of beginning again; they'd simply stopped what they were doing. They did not feel obliged to complete the plan and so they did not complete the plan. Just this, just these few details showed enough. And they must have really felt that and been quite satisfied with it, because why else would they have put these two dark fragments into such beautiful frames?

I've put them on the mantelpiece – you could say they've been given pride of place. They are close to one another but not exactly side by side: they are related, but they aren't a pair. Some people don't notice them at all and other people are instantly intrigued by them, in which case I go into the kitchen so they have every opportunity to become utterly absorbed without feeling obliged to talk about it, which would spoil everything. Yes, I could stand in the kitchen maybe and keep an eye on things from there and perhaps one day my heart by then will be right up in the roof of my mouth as I feel someone becoming more and more taken in until finally they call out to me, excited and amazed, and say, 'Look at that – she's been holding a parasol all along!'

There were so many flowers already in bloom when I moved in: wisteria, fuchsia, roses, golden chain, and many other kinds of flowering trees and shrubs I do not know the names of – many of them wild – and all in great abundance. The sun shone most days so naturally I spent most days out the front there, padding in and out all day long, and the air was absolutely buzzing with so many different species of bee and wasp, butterfly, dragonfly, and birds, so many birds, and all of them so busy. Everything: every plant, every flower, every bird, every insect, just getting on with it. In the mornings I flitted about my cottage, taking crockery out of the plate rack and organising it into jaunty stacks along the window ledge, slicing peaches and chopping hazelnuts, folding back the quilt and smoothing down the sheet, watering plants, cleaning mirrors, sweeping floors, polishing glasses, folding clothes, wiping casements, slicing tomatoes, chopping spring onions. And then, after lunch, I'd take a blanket up to the top garden and I'd lie down under the trees in the top garden and listen to things.

I would listen to a small beetle skirting the hairline across my forehead. I would listen to a spider coming through the grass towards the blanket. I'd listen to a squabbling pair of blue tits see-sawing behind me. I'd listen to the woodpigeon's wings whack through the middle branches of an ivy-clad beech tree and the starlings on the wires overhead, and the seagulls and swifts much higher still. And each sound was a rung that took me further upwards, and in this way it was possible for me to get up really high, to climb up past the clouds, towards a bird-like exuberance, where there is nothing at all but continuous light and acres of blue. Later on, towards evening, as it got cooler, I would snuggle into myself a little more and listen less and less so that, very slowly, I returned to dusk and earth. And then I'd soon begin to feel very hungry indeed so I'd sling the blanket across one shoulder and head back up to the cottage to start dinner. Which would frequently involve broad beans, lemons, perhaps some spinach, and plenty of chopped walnuts and white cheese.

Chopping.
Morning, noon and night, it seems.
How I love to chop.

Within these deep stone walls the sound of a large knife pounding against the chopping board is often mellow and euphonious; like a lulling chant it charms and placates me. Other times, late evening especially, the blade's keen reverberation is more rugged and insistent and I have to make a concerted effort to keep my eyes down and my hands steady. I go on with my guillotining and methodically pare down this robust gathering of swanky solanums until they lose colour. Chopping, taking it all to pieces, in a kind of contracted stupor, morning, noon and night; trying not to pay any heed to my reflection in the mirror as I do so. I can't stand that – above all I can't stand to see the reflection of my waist, winding back and forth, there in the mirror just to my right – looking as if it might take flight when I know very well it can't.

The Darkest Place in England

Lavinia Greenlaw

THE PEOPLE WHO COME looking for the dark tell Jamie she's lucky to live under such skies. Yes, she says, but Jamie is fifteen and desperate for brightness. She finds it in the stories she reads and the series she watches. Life, she thinks, is something she gets to observe. It takes no notice of her.

Jamie's father runs a farmshop and café on the edge of the moor. When tourists started turning up at dusk, wearing campaign t-shirts and asking for maps, he put up a sign: *Welcome to the Darkest Place in England*. The locals thought it was a joke. They were baffled when the tourists kept arriving and then they were impressed.

Men tell Jamie facts about light pollution and she's polite but she knows it all already. Her father has covered the café walls with campaign posters and pictures taken from space. She's surprised that

43

despite all the light the world can conjure, there's still so much darkness out there.

She's pretty in a way that makes some of these men speak to her of dangerous things. A girl like you walking home alone is better off in the dark. Under streetlamps you might as well be in a shop window, there for the taking. If someone wants to break in then the security lights are letting them see how, aren't they? There you are, all alone with your cheap locks and loose bolts…

None of this scares her. Living in a dark place, Jamie wants to say, doesn't make life mysterious or secret or anything. Her mother is dead but she has her father and three older brothers and the neighbours have known her all her life. The house is busy and full.

One Saturday evening a man comes into the café carrying a large bunch of flowers. He asks for a cup of tea and a bottle of water, and stands there smiling a little. He is shockingly handsome, thirty or forty – a grown-up she thinks, a man of the world. He reaches into his pocket for his wallet and goes to lay the flowers down on the counter only he doesn't. He holds them out, this dazzling bunch of flowers, and he says, These are for you.

The flowers are in her arms. She wonders if she misheard and what she might say as he places the exact money on the counter, intensifies his smile for a second and is gone. She holds the flowers to her face. They are alien shades of orange and pink, and their leaves are spikes and twirls. Are they beautiful? Jamie can't tell.

When has she felt like this? Once, when a boy she sat next to at school reached down and stroked her calf. He barely touched her but a million tiny lights exploded beneath her skin. They met later in the corridor and he pushed her against the wall, pressing himself to her.

Send us a picture.

What of?

Well not your face.

He stepped back indignantly as if she'd been the one to force herself on him and walked off chanting in a tight little voice: What of? What of?

That had been a year ago and she knows now what of and regularly hates herself for having been so stupid. This evening there's thick cloud and no one in the café and time is refusing to pass but a stranger has given her a bunch of flowers. How can she hate herself now?

Jamie is about to text her friend Chloe to tell her about the flowers when she realises that the man will probably come back for them. So she waits and when the door opens again she has them ready only it's not him. It's a girl called Piper who is also fifteen but looks twenty and hasn't bothered with Jamie since they were at primary school.

Piper often stays with friends to work on this or that and her parents choose to believe her. She has a capacious silver bag that she carries everywhere and the café is where she gets ready for a night out. Usually she nods at Jamie and marches straight to the bathroom but tonight she stops and points at the flowers.

Where d'you get those then?

Some man. Jamie knows to shrug.

Right, says Piper.

It's as if this story is so familiar that it doesn't bear telling. She thinks for a moment and then makes a decision.

Got any money?

A bit.

Wanna come out?

You mean now?

Well I don't mean tomorrow morning.

Like this?

Jamie is wearing black jeans and a black t-shirt.

> We can sort that. Don't you shut this place up around now? Lock the door.

Jamie texts her father to say she is staying with Chloe.

A short black dress appears from the silver bag followed by a sparkly halterneck, studded ankle boots, a pair of towering sandals and a bottle of vodka. Piper assesses Jamie and passes her the halterneck and boots. They fit. The top drapes and clings. Her bare shoulders prickle. The vodka burns cleanly. She is transformed.

Piper sends and receives messages constantly and without comment as she zips up the tiny black dress and climbs into the sandals. She paints her face and glues on extravagant lashes. Her white hair falls in a flat sheet and her skin is the colour of peach plastic. She sprays perfume behind her ears, across her breasts and high between her legs.

Jamie borrows Piper's make-up. When she's finished Piper adds more black to her eyes and red to her lips, and backcombs her hair.

> How do I look?

Jamie tries to sound as if she doesn't care.

> You look... (Piper is feeling generous)...
> famous.

A message comes and they go outside to wait.
Jamie won't ask what they're waiting for. She
doesn't want to spoil this. When she shivers Piper
passes her the bottle of vodka, and then she's warm
and laughing with her friend.

She remembers the flowers. She can't leave them
for her father to find but she can't drop them off
at home because there's no time and her father
would ask why she wasn't staying at Chloe's. She
must remember to text Chloe.

> I've just got to get... I can't leave them...
> they'll be...

She rushes back into the café.

> You're not bringing the flowers! shouts
> Piper.

> How many bunches of flowers have you
> been given like this?

> For this moment, Jamie is sure of her
> ground.

> You're right, Piper concedes. They're pretty
> fucking unusual.

A car pulls up, full of boys. Piper, sit here. If you keep your fucking hands to yourself. Not much chance of that. Who's this then? Jamie. Jamie? Yeah, Jamie. She's shoved against a boy who seems to be already half out the window. He turns his head into her cloud of hair and asks what the hell is with the flowers? His mouth touches her neck as he speaks.

She got given them right? Piper snaps back.

What for?

Piper doesn't bother to answer. She's not interested in who gave Jamie the flowers or why. Jamie is there to be another girl and to watch Piper's evening happen.

They drive along the back lanes. Lights off! The boys shout as they approach a crossroads. The driver accelerates. Piper screams as they shoot across the junction, her scream becoming laughter, neither sounding real. The driver turns the music up so loud that Jamie is feeling rather than hearing it. He starts to switch off the lights as they go round corners. Flick! Trees and houses are blotted out. Flick! The hills and lanes that contain her are wiped away. How can they still be moving when there's nothing to travel towards and nothing to leave behind or pass by? Jamie isn't scared. She's fascinated.

The car swoops onto the main road and on into the city, lurching from red light to red light as the driver brakes and accelerates. They pull up at a junction and the car stops as if shaking something off. Jamie loses hold of the flowers which fall forward and the driver shouts at her to get those fucking things out the way. She grabs them back and the boy next to her takes them and holds them out the window. That's better.

There's a man beside them on a motorbike. He's taking no notice of the boy hanging out of the car but then the kid calls out Hey! These are for you! So the man takes the flowers. The boy is pleased that the man has gone along with the joke and when the lights change he holds out his hand for the flowers but the man has gone. The boy is astonished.

Fuck! He fucking took the fucking flowers!

Everyone's laughing and so Jamie tries not to mind. If she hadn't had the flowers, Piper wouldn't have spoken to her and she wouldn't be here now in a car full of boys, proper boys, the kind who talk like they know what they're doing and as if everything's been decided. This is more than anything she's known – more exciting, more frightening, more real. This is what matters, not the flowers. She's already stopped thinking about the man who gave them to her.

Who was he? Someone of 35 whose wife is an up-and-coming soprano. She had given a lunchtime recital and he had been driving her back to the city. When they pulled up outside the café, she said would he please get rid of the horrible bouquet that had been pressed upon her. He meant to ask the girl where he could chuck it but she stared at them with such longing that he offered them to her instead. His wife had been amused. What was the girl like? Jamie wears her name on a silver necklace but the man hadn't noticed it. He remembers the heavy black of her hair, her shifting prettiness, a guarded restlessness. I can't remember, he says.

The atmosphere in the car becomes businesslike. Vodka and beer are passed round and someone reaches into Jamie's bag and takes money from her purse to pay for her share. She doesn't mind. They arrive at the club and meet more friends. Piper dismisses the boys and splits up the girls.

> Remember the rules. Don't queue in groups of more than three, ditch the lads and don't smile.

It works. For Jamie, it's like stepping into the watched world. There are dozens of girls as shiny and defined as Piper. They place themselves carefully, and talk and watch and drink with extreme attention. The boys who are with them are tense and alert. They too have prepared every detail of themselves. The crowd concentrates around the long bar where a thousand drinks are poured. There's a deal on shots and Piper lines them up and passes them back to Jamie.

When Jamie turns towards the room, everything's slipped. Someone at a nearby table is crying. Boys slap and punch one another with only-joking smiles. Jamie makes her way to the toilets where her bag is searched and the cubicles have been stripped out. There's a row of girls pissing indifferently while others gather at the mirrors or round phones.

She finds Piper again and says something important but Piper can't hear and passes her a small clear drink. It's on fire. Jamie goes to swallow it down like everything else but Piper knocks it out of her hand and shrieks and Jamie feels proud to have entertained her. They grab a table and gather boys who compete to pull out money every time Piper's glass is empty. Jamie's head is folding in on itself but she keeps drinking. She's still waiting for something to happen. Eventually Piper pulls Jamie to her feet and they move onto the dancefloor.

Everything disappears and then appears again, and this is how it is for the next however many hours – like being cast up on the shore one minute and deep underwater the next. Jamie lets herself rise and fall. She feels so much that she feels nothing.

A boy appears in front of her and leans in to be heard.

You look quiet, he shouts.

I am quiet, she yells back.

He laughs and pulls her towards him but doesn't look at her again. His head tips back as his hands move round her waist, down over her hips. As he presses and rubs she moves with him. Her body is doing what it's supposed to do, without her having to think about it. The song ends and the boy leads her off the floor and into a part of the club where everything is soft and low. They turn a corner and Jamie sees Piper. She tells the boy she wants to get back to her friend who is… where? Over there. As she points, she sees a boy pull Piper onto his lap and start to pump her up and down.

Your friend's busy, the boy says. Come on.

He's pulling her through the crowd and while some small part of her is trying to resist, most of her is unable. Then she sees something that makes her stop – the bunch of flowers. They have been returned to her. My flowers! She says it to the boy but he has continued on and doesn't hear her.

Three brunettes are sitting in a row watching the room. Beside them is an empty chair and on it, the flowers. As soon as Jamie tries to concentrate she finds it impossible to move but she is tall in Piper's studded boots and she pushes slowly towards the chair and picks up the flowers.

What the fuck?

One of the brunettes leaps up and snatches them back.

The others stand up too. They are all, like Jamie, uncertain on their feet. The first brunette waggles a finger in Jamie's face.

Bitch tried to nick my flowers! She shouts at the room.

Jamie opens her mouth to explain. These are her flowers. See? The twirls and spikes, the pinks and oranges. She doesn't know that hundreds of identical bunches are sold each day and that a DJ gave this one to this girl as a prize for doing something that the boys cheered the loudest. These are not Jamie's flowers.

He gave them to me, Jamie manages at last. To me.

Another brunette raises a hand so sharply that Jamie flinches but all she does is push back a wing of hair so that Jamie can see her outrage more clearly. Jamie is frightened but these are her first flowers, her only flowers, and now that she has found them she's not going to lose them again. She tries to grab them, the brunettes are yelling and other people join in.

She didn't do nothing!

It was the other one!

She's off her head! She just walked over and took the flowers!

Jamie is moved through the crowd and along a dark corridor as if she were no more than a bunch of flowers herself. A door opens and she is placed quite gently beyond it. She tries to work out where she is but the world is thick forest. The sky seems to sit just over her head and in whatever direction she moves there are black branches. The branches tangle, something pushes, something pulls, and she falls. The world closes.

The club is emptying now and for all the noise everyone is making, most are too drunk to be anything other than marooned in themselves. There are boys who curl into their own shadows and girls dressed for a fairytale summer who lie down as if they've wandered into a soft green clearing where someone will watch over them till morning.

Into the forest come the three brunettes. They are practiced at this and know to link arms and how to get home. They step precisely over vomit, blood and glass and turn away from a girl slumped against a wall who cannot raise her head as one boy engineers her legs and another takes pictures. The three brunettes turn a corner and there in a side-street they find Jamie. She is on her back, her head tipped to one side, her arms outstretched. They totter and giggle and the one with the flowers steps forward. She lays them on Jamie's chest and folds her hands around them. Have the fucking flowers, she says. They each take a picture and then they walk on.

Someone else stops. He has passed other girls lying in the street but this one is different. She's holding a bunch of flowers. It's the girl from the café lying in the street at two in the morning. What has he done? He thinks she must be here because he gave her the flowers – which is true, she is. He does not know that these are not those flowers.

His wife has a migraine and he has just driven to the city's one all-night chemist. His car is just round the corner and he could be home in ten minutes but here is the girl. He stopped and now he has to do something. He bends down and puts a hand to her cheek. Jamie opens her eyes and he helps her sit up. She stares at him and then at the flowers. She's still in the argument with the three brunettes.

They're my flowers.

Yes, he says as if to a child, your flowers.

He brings her to her feet as if he's about to dance her down the road and then turns to walk away but she lurches, doubles up and starts to vomit. She's a young girl who can't stand up. He cannot leave her.

Where are your friends?

She shakes her head.

Where do you live?

She opens her mouth and closes it again.

Near the café? Where you work?

She nods and now he has to drive her home. They set off to his car where he helps her into the seat, wipes her face and tucks his jacket around her.

What's your name?

She doesn't reply.

It must be nice living on the moor.

She murmurs something.

Dark, sure. Anything else?

Nothing else.

The girl dozes the rest of the way and seems almost sober when she gets out. She hasn't made a mess of his car or asked him his name. He's free to go.

When Jamie wakes up, her heart is ticking. Somewhere within the pain in her head are the details of what happened. She remembers the car ride, the flaming drink, the rise and fall of the dancefloor, a hand on her waist, the boy hard against her. The way her body hurts is not like being ill, she thinks, it's like experience, which is what Jamie wants so much. The flowers that are not her flowers are lying beside her.

She goes to work in the café. Piper comes by and Jamie tries to explain what happened but Piper isn't interested. She's only there to pick up her boots and top. Jamie thinks that everything should be different only it isn't. She's still waiting for something to happen.

A week later, Piper walks into the café with her silver bag and they do it all again. This time when Jamie is led off the dancefloor and up the stairs, there are no flowers to divert her. She does it again and again, for the rush through the dark and the press of boys and the push of the music and the rise and fall within herself. She loses sight of Piper. Your friend's a mess, someone says to Piper as they watch Jamie being rotated round the dancefloor by two boys who are taking it in turn to grapple with her breasts. Who? Piper says.

Piper stops turning up at the café but Jamie now has numbers punched into her phone. She buys her own silver bag, fills it with vodka and catches the one bus that passes by on a Saturday evening. These nights end in the forest where the things that happen don't have to be felt. Someone puts her in a car and she's dropped back at the bus stop on the main road from where she walks down the sunken lane that leads into the village.

She watches the car sink away as night rises up around her and sets off downhill. When there's no moon, she can't see the lane beneath her feet. It's like walking on the surface of nothing. When she reaches the first houses, she attempts to stride. Sometimes she sings a broken song. Those who catch sight of her might mention it to others – or not. After all, what are they themselves doing up at 3am? No one says anything to Jamie's father. He has brought up four children alone and carries great sadness.

In November, when it's pouring with rain, one of her teachers drives past and thinks to offer her a lift but he's learnt to fear such creatures. When there's frost on the ground, the woman who sits up all night waiting for someone she can no longer name, watches over the girl for the moment she passes. One night in December, Jamie is walking home when it starts to snow. She's entranced by how sudden and total this snowfall is. The world is breaking down – the trees, the telegraph poles, the lane – but so very softly! She looks up and sees that the snow is going to fall forever and when she looks around her again, she sees that everything has become snow. Standing there on the edge of the moor in the middle of the night watching such gentleness take shape is just the unasked-for experience she has been hoping for. Something has happened at last.

She will be discovered in a field close to home, looking as if she lay down on a summer's night in a soft green clearing. She will survive this, but for now let her sleep. The place where she sleeps is neither light nor dark. Every hour someone comes to check on her breathing. Machines flicker and blip. Time piles up like snow.

People gather to tell stories about how they saw her and wanted to save her. Let them say now what they knew, having said nothing. Her teacher recalls that he offered her a lift, which she declined. Boys delete messages and pictures. The three brunettes tell everyone they know her and they cry. When a teacher tells Piper that Jamie has woken up and is going to be alright, Piper asks Who?

The man who gave Jamie the flowers might have seen the stories in the paper but they were just a few lines about how she was found and how she would recover. He may not have seen them at all but he remembers Jamie.

One evening he drives to the café (why?) and goes in. There she is. He asks for tea and lingers but Jamie is sending and reading messages continuously and barely looks up. Should he have brought her more flowers?

That night he plays a song he hasn't listened to for years and sends a message to his college sweetheart. That's what he calls her to himself – my sweetheart – and then he writes it. How are you, sweetheart? He remembers the shock and joy of her body. I've been wondering, he writes and then hesitates.

He sits for an hour, playing the song, and then deletes the unsent message and goes to bed beside his wife where he lies awake, thinking nothing, while the stars pile up overhead.

In a Right State

Hilary Mantel

'We sit there, slowly doing the quick crossword, noting as so often in institutions the presence of characters who seem habitués, knowing the procedures, familiar with the staff, A&E their scene.'

- Alan Bennett,
London Review of Books, January 2016.

IN THE DAYS WHEN I had a reading lamp, I'd sit down with the papers at the weekend and make up answers to celebrity quizzes. Tell us your favourite food and who you despise. If a fire broke out, what would you save? The celebrities say, my loved one, my Persian cat, my grandmother. They mean, it would depend in which of my houses I was resident at the time.

The quizzes never ask you what you'd save if you were evicted. They ask, what would your superpower be? I say, getting my furniture back from those conniving bastards.

On the day of my turn-out the men were polite. I have no complaints about their manners. They gave me no choice of timing or any other choice, so you need your plans in advance, no use thinking what to save when they're pounding up the stairs. You've got two bags, when it comes down to it. You've seen these bags. They're very nearly un-bags, faint-striped as though they've been through a car wash. Because they have no shape, they can't get shapeless with use, so you can't get more depressed by them than you already are. Pack your stuff inside and the handles cut into your fingers. That's not the injury that brings me to the hospital, but then again it is. Cut fingers, broken hearts, glue ears and tennis elbow: they all go in the same door. I say to a woman as I take a seat, 'Whatever happened to tennis elbow? You never hear of it any more.'

'Nor boils,' another customer says. 'People don't have boils like back in the day. It must be because we're better vitaminised. Still, never say never, with boils. They could come back. Same as TB.'

'Gout's back,' a man in the corner whispers.

Another says, 'What happened to Chinese Restaurant Syndrome? You heard of that at one time.'

'MSG,' a woman says.

'That too,' a man says. 'It's what I'm here for.'

It's hardly out of his mouth before a lass has her phone out, googling. A few people edge away. The rows are filling up, so they can't go far. If we were celebrities and anyone asked us, we'd say this was our favourite place in the world. If they asked, 'What is the first thing you remember?' we'd say, 'Being here.'

Are you sick? In pain? Yes. Right, sit there. Fine, now wait. Name?

Oh, don't start that, I say.

A man says, 'It's looking like four hours, except for the lucky few.'

I ponder it. 'The fast lane. I don't think that would be a good thing.'

'At least we're out of this filthy weather.'

'I've not seen you before,' I say. 'Are you poorly?'

He says, do you think I come here for a hobby, like BMX bikes or growing dahlias?' But then he relents. He likes someone to be interested in him. 'It's a rodent ulcer,' he says. 'It's an old-fashioned sort of a thing, but I've got it.'

'Ah, Jesus!' a woman says. 'That sounds terrible. Where is it? What do they do for it?'

'Private,' he says. 'They'll have to dig it out.'

That'll be histology, we say, looking at each other. Tests. They're not going to scrape it out and send you on your merry way. You should come back when it's quiet. Unless you've nothing better to do.

'Oh, pardon me,' he says. 'Pardon me, for having a lethal condition on a Friday night. What an idiot.'

He sounds bitter.

'Be honest,' I say. 'What have you planned for tomorrow?'

'I thought in terms of dying,' he says. 'At your sodding convenience, of course.'

I tell him, there's no point showing up at twilight, with complexities like yours. You get better attention in the forenoon. After that you have to give way to the regulars, who know how to push themselves up the order. Habitués. The kind who roll on the floor and fake peritonitis. Who bring their own supper.

Time passes. Ron pulls out his pack of cards and deals his mates in. Rodent's not part of the inner circle. Neglected, he begins to swivel his eyes around. He shuffles his feet, he huffs and puffs, he's getting ready to explode: I read the signs. Another minute and 'Oi! Oi!' he shouts. 'Is nobody paying me any attention? I'm in agony here.'

'You should try gout,' says the quiet man in the corner. He is daffodil pale, his head lolls, his stick trembles in his hands and a coffee from the machine has gone down his cardigan. Somehow it's impossible to look at him without the question bubbling to your lips, 'How often do you have sex?'

An hour gone. 'Slow,' a woman says. 'I'm not complaining, just saying.' Sombrely she hand-gels herself, like jesting Pilate. Ron licks his pencil and takes an order for Greggs, jotting it on the back of the ace of spades. He pulls up his collar, heads out: *hasta la vista*, say the habitués, and settle to their sudoku. It seems we have a long, quiet night ahead.

There are times when you can smell an incident in the air, feel its vibration before it strikes – a distant mutter of human voices, like a riot coming down the road. The red telephones shrill, the staff sprint, simple souls are slammed to the wall. There are bubble-wrapped bodies on flying trolleys, intubation and vomit, a tang of saline, sweat and machine oil: and all the red of the world fills your eye, the casualties swathed in crimson, the scarlet casing of fire bells behind glass. But tonight is a space for the connoisseurs of small, strange pains: for inexplicable rashes and three-day headaches, for doors swinging and gusting in a sour chill, with rain in the wind and no prospect of better.

Over on the left they are playing Desert Island Discs, but in our segment silence prevails. I cast about for general remarks. Often you can animate a whole room with the popular question, 'Chocolate or cheese?' But the habitués have all stated their preference and will stick to it. 'What single thing,' I venture, 'would improve the quality of your life?'

'If I could stop throwing up,' a woman says.

'If you could stop doing it in public,' says the man with her.

'Yes, that would be nice.' The woman looks thoughtful, and green. 'Or not on other people's feet,' she says.

All the people sweep their feet under their chairs. The rodent says, 'If only I had something for the pain! I wish I had a herbal remedy.' He looks at me. 'You got a bit of herbal remedy in your pocket?'

'Not got a pocket,' I say.

The people join in. 'Leave her alone! Anybody can see she's not got a pocket.'

I try to read the paper but it doesn't take. I don't fault the news but I've read it before. I shuffle through looking for puzzles and quizzes. Somebody has filled in the quick crossword, got halfway through and then – what? Died? 'Quick but not quick enough!' I say. I show the paper around.

They call me. You want to get into this gown, they say. It barely covers half of me and you never know, do you, is it leave the front open, or the back? Each time, I'll get into it and somebody will come through the curtain and stand there snorting: 'Look at you!'

Burn me up with humiliation.

I always think, I'll know next time, I'll remember. But I never do.

I lugged my bags into the cubicle because I didn't feel safe to leave them. You don't want to leave them with a man with a gnawing ailment, in case it's gnawing his brain – he looks respectable, but then so did my old man when he'd shaved, and I've heard of cases where the controls go out of whack, so the right hand doesn't know what the left hand is doing. Picture it: his left hand is scuffing up *Hello!* magazine and pointing to hats worn by Princess Eugenie, while his right is pilfering my remaining possessions.

As I was going through the curtain, a bloke came up right behind me. 'Up you go, granny!' He meant to be helpful, but I was on the couch before I was ready. *What is your favourite direction, up or down?* I was wearing the gown with the gap at the back. That was my decision – and as I was sitting on my bottom, I felt at no great disadvantage. My bare legs dangled over the sides of the couch. 'Just shove my stuff under,' I said. 'Then it won't be in anybody's way.'

I would have done it myself but I didn't want to get down again and show my bottom. *What is your most embarrassing moment?* Time passed. A man pulled the curtain back. Could be porter, could be doctor, all look the same in blue coveralls. He shouts to somebody over his shoulder, 'She's in a right state.'

I say, Is that a diagnosis or a location?

'Jesus, what's these?' He's nearly fallen over my bags. 'That's a trip hazard,' he says. 'Safety in the workplace.'

I say, That young fellow out there has a rodent disorder. Why don't you cease pontificating and go out and stop him, before he goes on a rampage? The sight of so many hats has driven him mad.

'You seem to know my job,' he says. (I knew by this he was the doctor; it's not what the porters say, they have different things they say.) Blimey, I say, I should do! Know your job? I was for twenty years the leading government surgeon to the vice-president of the Seychelles. I dare say you know that gentleman, and he will vouch for me. Ring him up. Get him on the blower.

'Sit there,' he says, 'and don't move.'

I sit. *What is your chief regret?* It's that I don't say all I think, or think all I say: a general regret, I'm sure. I do as I'm told and don't move. My legs go dead, dangling down. In the days when I had a motor vehicle, we'd bowl along singing: we'd come to a sign that said 'Diversion,' and we'd shout, 'It might be all right for some, but it's not what I'd call entertainment!'

Within an hour, they part the curtains and come at me with a sanity quiz. 'Do you know the name of the Prime Minister?'

I burst out laughing. I slap my bare thigh, it's all I'm allowed to slap. What's funny? they ask. I say, if you don't know that, son, you're not fit to have the vote.

I try in vain to explain my talk was not so random as they experienced it. It comes out of my mouth in reasonable order, I say, only your understanding is defective. A blower, I explain, is an old-fashioned term for a telephone: no, I don't know why either. This vice-president, somebody says, is he on Facebook? Is it where you've went for your holiday?

'Maybe,' I say. 'Mahé.'

'You'd see how she got the idea,' a porter or doctor exclaims. 'All those curling-up travel magazines out there in the waiting area.'

Only he calls it a bagging area, because he's tired.

Outside the curtain, a savoury smell goes by. It's the second round of Steak Bakes coming in. My mouth waters. They pump up my blood pressure. 'One-eighty on top,' he says. 'Not too clever.'

'I see that,' I say, 'but you shouldn't feel badly. We can't all be gifted or special.'

He writes on my form. I think he wants to write 'facetious' but he can't spell it.

It's after midnight. Go out as bidden. Take seat. The man with gout praying in a quiet, unobtrusive way. Slipped sideways in her seat, the green woman sleeps.

In the days when I had a licence, I'd see people like this on TV: rag-tags of the social disorder. The rodent's seat is empty and I wonder if he's been carried away by his own fiction. Gout hesitates: 'Gents, I think.'

'Right,' I say. 'Making a night of it.'

Sure enough, when he comes back, his face is red and his eyes rolling. He's taken something but I don't like to say what and I'm sure he doesn't either.

'Oi, you!' He stands over me. 'Who do you think you are, calling me a thief? I never stole anything smaller than a fridge.'

I say. 'You'd steal the pencil from a polling booth. It's your sort that got this lot elected.'

Have you noticed, you never meet anybody who admits to voting for them? 'No, not my fault,' they claim. 'I tried to vote for the other lot, but somebody had moved the pencil. Next time, I'll get a postal. Because,' they say smugly, 'I've got an address.'

After a while I put down my paper. I say, what would you save first if a flood broke out?

The woman says, without opening her eyes, 'My ark.'

'Good answer,' I say.

The rodent looks up. 'Your wok? What's the point of that?'

I say, 'Save your dove and your olive branch too.' The time will come when you get tired of that vast taffeta sea and the occluded light, nothing but ripples to the horizon: tired of the gentle rocking of the world beneath you, nostalgic for the time you could stand upright without flexing yourself against a mast.

'Bloody beansprouts,' the rodent says. 'Arsing about with water chestnuts, in a case of national emergency? Sod off!'

'It's not national,' somebody says. 'Only us.'

'It's only in here,' Gout says.

'We could be in this queue till next year,' says MSG. 'Then we'd be in the Guinness Book of Records.'

'Do they still have that?' Gout says. 'Or has it gone the way of all flesh?'

Rodent sits up. 'Hello! Looking lively!'

Some staff scurry past, name tags flapping. Plastic aprons snap the air. Somebody runs a drip stand through. A couple of trolleys trundle into the corridor. A sound of retching from the blanketed heaps. 'Could be norovirus.' MSG says. 'Could be hantavirus. Could be tropical, we're swamped with immigrants, you never know what they're bringing in.'

'Give over,' Ron says to him. 'Are you MSG, or BNP? Or are you just MD? That's mentally deficient,' Ron says, before the googling starts up. 'But you can't say that these days, you have to say… I dunno.' Ron blows his nose. 'I lose count.'

You hear about hospitals being clogged up with casualties from fights. It's a little-known fact that most of these fights start in A&E itself, with insults flying about Munchausen's Syndrome, and old hands ridiculing the new boys and laughing at their bandages. That's when the staff wade in and you get a porter with a fat lip, and crackling radios and flying clipboards and Plod pitching in. It's when you go over the four-hour target that folk start to squabble. Tonight I don't need to ask the time to see the mark's been missed. It's clear to the habitué that the system has broken down and they're all running about without a plan.

Nobody trusts the breakdown services these days. I used to wonder how you had a breakdown. Even if you've broken inside, how do you demonstrate it, do you lie on the floor and scream? In that case, how is it distinguishable from normal behaviour? It depends on your age, it was put to me. If you're under three and over ninety, okay. Anything in between, it indicates a loss of self-esteem. You're in the way of the mopping, besides. Some supermarket spillage, soup or blood or butter, and before you can say, 'It wasn't me,' a bell shrills: the cleaners are charging in with their yellow signs on legs, DANGER: MOPPING IN PROGRESS. You're lying in the aisle in the broken glass impeding the flow of shoppers. What's the matter, they say, has she had a breakdown? Try and get her to the side of the aisle, in the special lane. Just filter around her, that's the way. Move along now. Nothing to see.

In the days when I drove a car, we'd see people on the motorway, speeding along with a canoe strapped on their roof rack. We'd shout, blimey, does he work for the Met Office, does he know something we don't know? You'd see cars with two bikes perched on top: we used to shout, would you look at those pessimists? We'd put the window down and call, 'My man, did you ever think of joining the AA?'

But that was when we were plural, young and bold. If we got our heads punched in for being cheeky, all in a day's work.

It's 1am. I get out my Q&A: an old one, no matter. 'Here's one that will have you all going. What was the best kiss of your life?'

Rodent says, 'She's getting on my wick. Can't somebody stop her? She's been unspooling this nonsense for the last hour.'

The green woman snaps her eyes open and says, 'What would you consider a reasonable length of time?'

'It speaks!' says her partner. 'Watch your feet!'

I notice the row of feet have crept out from under the chairs. Now they flip back, a single movement like a chorus line. The rodent gets up. He goes to the desk. I can't hear what he's saying but he turns to me and jerks his thumb, and the woman behind the desk glances over but then she just talks on her phone, wheeling back and forth on her tall chair, and the rat goes on thumbing, and she goes on socially excluding him, till one of us shouts up from the seats, For God's sake, you're blocking the aisle up, there's people dying in here and you're taking all the room.

The habitués on the desert island are singing 'Hi Ho Silver Lining'. But when they see the rumpus they break off and start shouting too.

I want to get home now. It's three in the morning. My transport options are limited. The woman on the desk says, we can call you a cab, we have a number. What's the name again?

I tell her and she does a complete whirl on her chair. 'Come again?'

Taxi company don't like it either, I say. I explain I have special names for cab purposes. You get tired of their switchboard going, 'How are you spelling it?': as if you had options. So you say, 'Smith. Car for Smith, please.' *What would your ideal surname be?* When they turn up – if they bother – they say, 'Smith, eh? I seen Smiths in my time and Madam, you no Smith. You don't sound like Smith, you don't smell like Smith, you don't get in this cab, because this cab, it is Smiths only. And by the way,' they say, 'if you want to try some trick, don't try that Smith trick. Because lady, you are deeply unconvincing.'

I start gathering my things together. The un-bags. My coat. The rodent says, 'Given up then? Younger generation. No stamina!' He's jeering at me. 'Here.' He holds out the raggedy newspaper. 'Take your quick crossword and fuck off.'

I say, I can't make it come out if I sit over it till doomsday. Some moron has scribbled in the blanks. Probably that doctor, he's not too clever.

'Well, just wrap yourself in the paper,' the man says, 'and go and sit outside. You're too late for the night bus.' He turns to the green woman. 'And you're insane, too! Wok? Wok my arse! What's the use of soy sauce, with the country under water?'

'I'm going,' I say. 'They're turning me out. It appears a "Smiths Only" policy has come in.'

Gout breaks off his prayer. He looks at me blearily and grips his stick. 'Don't do anything I wouldn't do.'

I pick up my gear and put it down again. I can't quite make up my mind to the morning. I might have failed with the crossword but I don't like to go with questions hanging in the air. What is your idea of a perfect weekend? Have you ever said I love you, and not meant it? I ask the green woman, 'What is your greatest fear?'

'That man,' she says. 'The one who complained. I'm afraid he'll complain about me next.'

'Oh, why so?' her partner says. 'Aren't you the

sort of company we all crave on a big night out, throwing up on people's evening shoes?'

Spew if you must, I say, but never fear. You could be in a right state, but instead you are here. Remember, we have a government that took on the badgers. They stood up to the terror waged by those black and white bastards. They went for them in their very setts, they sniffed them out like Osama Bin Laden.

'Write your answers down,' I say, 'and keep them in your sleeves. Sit tight, and I'll see you all tomorrow.'

I used to go on a straight path. I knew the route through my days from A to B. Somewhere along the way, I tripped on my own bags, I slipped on my own mopping. I went to a fantasy dinner party with General Custer and Virginia Woolf, and I never came home again, or else when I came home they'd moved it.

It must be dawn soon, if it weren't winter. I get my gloves on – or perhaps somebody else's, you get your fingers mixed up at my age – and I make my way to the entrance. I walk away from the light of the blue screens and towards the search for a breakfast. The glass doors swoosh open and let me into the cold. Outside there's an area for ambulances, criss-crossed against the tarmac: KEEP CLEAR AT ALL TIMES. If only, I say. I shout it out loud as I walk; when it's this early, the streets are yours to shout in. Tell us a secret, the papers say: tell us a joke. I say, if you're short of a joke look around you. *Circumspice,* as I used to say: in the days when I had an education.

Disappearances

K J Orr

September 18, Buenos Aires

THE BEGINNING IS SIMPLE enough: I find myself in
the park due to a sudden and overwhelming urge to
go to the museum.

People speak of the shock of retirement. They warn
of the possibility of profound depression. However,
this is not something I expect for myself. The life I
have built here over the years keeps me more than
occupied, regardless of work. And so it comes as a
surprise to me – this nervous and shifty feeling on
waking. It is as if I can only sidle up to the day, like
a neurotic suitor.

My restlessness increasingly translates itself into
abrupt impulses. To put it bluntly, an urge presents
itself much in the manner of the need to urinate or
defecate, and demanding immediate action. It is due
to just such an impulse that I find myself on the
steps of the museum at an absurdly early hour
without any real justification for being there.

The museum – established many years ago, and in part with my family's money – houses a moderate collection of European art, mostly paintings, some sculpture, in a building of national importance warranting both attention and preservation. It is a while since I've been there. Not since '93 perhaps.

It is closed, of course. Everywhere is closed at this time of day.

I consider my options. I could return to the apartment. Carolina will be there soon enough to make my coffee and breakfast. However I have woken to a clear sky and it remains fine. It has been neither a long walk nor an unpleasant one, passing through the park. Under the circumstances I decide to walk on.

The jacarandas are coming into bloom. It is spring – and early enough in the day to find some moments of peace before the city's traffic starts spewing noise and fumes.

I find myself gravitating to the edge of the park in the hope of locating a newspaper stand before heading for home.

It is odd how places local to us can remain invisible for so long – until one day they simply present themselves.

The café sits directly on the corner of what is, by day, a busy avenue. It is set back however, separated by railings, a broad curve of paving stones, and the beginnings of a long colonnade.

I cross the avenue and look in. I see a mahogany bar and small, round tabletops. There is no one in sight.

I try the door; it opens. I enter, and take a seat.

From my table I can see the park opposite, with its careful beds of colour, its gravelled paths and ornamental fountains.

As I wait, I watch light enter through the deco windows that overlook the colonnade. I watch greens and reds and blues from the stained glass play across the black and white tiling on the floor. They meddle with its orderly geometry.

I glance up and see a woman standing behind the bar. I have not been aware of her. She wears a pressed white shirt, a long black apron tied tight about her waist.

'*Cafecito, por favor.*'

When she serves me I notice her hands.

*

It becomes a habit. I spend every morning at the café, at the same table, served always by the same woman. She is the only person working there at this hour.

I wake myself up every day at five. It becomes automatic, no need for an alarm. I throw on clothes, and head out. I stroll in the park – without fail I go to the museum. I stand on the steps, look up at the door – it is always closed, the museum always shut. I observe the building for a few moments, and walk on. I trace my path beside the row of jacarandas.

At the edge of the park I cross the avenue. I look through the window of the café before entering and sitting in my usual spot.

The first morning I order my coffee in Spanish and every morning afterwards I do the same. This is unusual. Both in my line of work and in my social life I have been most used to speaking English – other than for that period at the start of the '80s. I was schooled in England and trained for my profession there, so the language is habitual. It would be accurate to say that by and large I reserve the use of Spanish for communication with Carolina, and other help.

I might also mention that the clothes I am wearing on the first day I continue to wear every day, at this hour. I dress in haste – and while I do not quite head out in night attire the general effect cannot be far off. I am not one given to wearing sporting clothes outside the home, but a tracksuit is near enough the truth. I look as though I might have been speed-walking, for health. Suffice to say that according to my usual standards I am unrecognisable.

Now, therefore, I find myself each day close to home, in my neighbourhood, but at an hour when no one I know is about. I do not look as I usually would. I do not speak as I usually do.

The moment anyone else enters the café, I leave.

The rest of my day continues as before. I go home. I shower. I change into something more appropriate. Carolina has my breakfast prepared, as ever. I spend the day in social engagements.

I have spoken of my retirement as something unnerving, but I am not to be pitied. I live in the city's most expensive district. My work introduced me to the wealthiest and most beautiful of Buenos Aires. I made them more beautiful under my knife; they made me wealthier. I was adopted into their circle, popular for my skills as a surgeon, but also for a family history woven through the streets in plaques and memorials: a flawless pedigree.

It is in truth quite some time since I've paid much attention to family. As a young man in the fifties, I longed to be rid of the burden of their decency. I could not bear the thought of following their traditions, their moral imperatives, faithfully treading the path of generations like a mule. I had inherited a good mind, and after some years of training in Oxford, England, I qualified as a surgeon, only to turn my hand to facelifts. I considered myself very clever indeed. I believe I was in pursuit of something perverse – the more vulgar the better. I returned to Buenos Aires and set up shop on home turf to make an exhibition of myself. The family were appalled of course, and I stopped seeing them.

It was a game. I took pleasure in playing the subversive. It suited me well.

The waitress asks me what I do for a living.

I laugh. I'm an old man. I'm retired.

She persists. She wants to know.

This is not a conversation I want to have. I enjoy being a stranger. I like this woman knowing nothing of my life, or who I am. I would like to keep it that way.

But it's the first sign of interest she has shown me, and it would be rude not to respond. Our relationship until now – though largely mute – has been a thing of pleasure. It's hard to explain.

I pause before speaking. I can say anything. I can say I was a poet. I was a road sweeper. I was a baker. I was an architect. She'll never know.

I thrived. It didn't matter who was in charge – throughout the decades, through all the ins and outs, the various shenanigans our country went through. While the leadership had wives and mistresses I was in demand. And while I have never possessed matinée idol looks, I flatter myself that I was their Hephaestus – these women love being done by an ugly man if he is craftsman to the gods.

I tell her I was a surgeon. I am not more specific than that.

I think it will end there, our chat, but she interprets what I say – she assumes I was a general surgeon, and goes on to tell me about the man who saved her brother's life when she was eight, at the time her father disappeared. Of course, not everyone has had my easy run through the years.

Her eyes are warm as she relates this tale, nonetheless. She even takes a seat on the chair across from mine. When she has finished – the story is not long, but quite moving – she studies me in open admiration.

I know that I can end it there and then. A couple of words would suffice. But I don't.

She holds out her hand and shakes mine, solemnly – as if we have some pact – before standing, putting the chair back in position, and resuming work.

I remain at my table. I finish my coffee. I retain the sensation of the smooth swell of scar tissue I felt against my palm as she took my hand. Not burns as I had first thought, but what must have been deep lacerations, horizontal, on both of her palms.

I think to myself, again: What does it matter? What does it matter what she thinks I did, the sort of man she imagines I have been?

When I get up to leave she stops what she's doing and smiles at me from behind the bar.

'I'm Beatriz,' she says.

I maintain the illusion she's created. It's not hard. If she likes thinking of me as some sort of hero, should I stop her? I like these mornings, and am loath to disrupt them. I like the silent agreement, the way she mostly ignores me, works around me. And she obviously admires the work she thinks I have done.

Our mornings continue. The days are warm. The jacarandas bloom like fists unfurling underneath clear skies.

Irene Varela-Morales. She is an acquaintance – in her fifties. She doesn't see me sitting in the corner, and I have no particular wish to be seen.

I gave her a noble nose. It improved things immeasurably and she's well aware of it. She carries herself in such a way that her profile is always seen to full advantage.

Irene stands impatiently – though making sure she's side-on to the approaching waitress – unwilling, it seems, either to take a seat or stand by the bar. There is a brief exchange – she doesn't look at my Beatriz – and then she takes a table near the door. She faces away from the bar, towards the street.

Beatriz leaves to fulfil the order she has been given but is called back. Irene stands, and – visibly irritated, still side-on, without looking at Beatriz – casts her wrap across the table, into her face, with great force. Such is her surprise, and the speed with which it is slung, that it is all Beatriz can do to catch the thing before it slips to the floor.

She takes it, smooths it, hangs it on the stand beside the door. Irene could have done it herself. The stand is right there.

Beatriz says nothing. She returns to the bar.

Soon she is back at the table, putting down a coffee, milk and water, with a plate of *medialunas*.

The moment she has gone Irene calls her

back. She speaks in English with a phoney American drawl. She says, 'I don't want that,' of the *medialunas*, and 'I asked for hot milk. Take this back.'

Beatriz doesn't answer. She looks at the jug that Irene's holding out. '*Leche. Caliente*,' Irene says slowly.

Beatriz goes back to the bar and, moments later, returns with another jug.

'It really shouldn't be this complicated,' Irene says. She speaks first in English and then follows it with Spanish.

She plays this game a good while.

More water.

Ice.

Another spoon.

A clean one.

Beatriz adjusts the awning over the windows outside – the sun is in Irene's eyes.

When she departs, she doesn't leave a tip.

It is true that the people can be rude here in Recoleta, where there is so much money. The very wealthy too often forget their manners – maybe because they have no cause to remember them. Often they give the impression that it is not forgetfulness at all but clear intention that makes them do it, a kind of assertion of their greater importance in the world; a ruse of sorts that often works – at the very least, superficially.

I see it in Beatriz's face.

It is true that many of them are my neighbours

– these people are the sort of people I have
known, my friends, even; though I have had no
reason to discuss this with her. We have set the
parameters of our acquaintance.

She pulls out the chair that sits across from me a
second time. She lights a cigarette.

'When they want to take their time, they
take their time,' she says. 'When they want to get
out of here quickly, they do. They want what they
want and they make it known. "This is what I
want. This is not what I want. What is this? This
is *not* what I ordered. Get the manager – my maid
called to reserve and this idiot didn't write it
down." These people – they throw their money at
you. They never look you in the eye. They like to
assume that you are stupid. Maybe it's more fun
that way.'

She shrugs. She stubs out her cigarette, and
then she gives me that smile. 'These people,' she
says.

I don't know how to respond. I reach across
the table to take a sip of coffee but somehow –
my hand is trembling, it's been happening of late
– I spill it. 'Stupid,' I say. 'I'm so sorry.'

'They have been working hard, these hands.
Give them a break,' she says.

She takes my hand between her palms.

I cannot remember whether my acquaintance
with Irene was simply professional, or more. I
have been acquainted with a number of women.

The term 'acquaintance' is undoubtedly correct. I have not been one for long alliances.

I was married – once – an odd, abortive affair.

I have been so used to unravelling women, peeling back their faces, constantly imagining them into something other than they are.

It is not that I have not enjoyed them – far from it – but they are no more or less than the sum of their parts.

It's natural.

Irene Varela-Morales returns to the café. She brings a friend, Valentina – I forget, but I think the surname is Suarez.

They assault my table.

'I told you he was hiding out in this place.'

She claims she spotted me from the first – *knew* she recognised me, but couldn't place me in those *ghastly* clothes.

Valentina launches herself. 'Look at you! I can't *believe* you thought you'd get away with it!'

'What a bad, bad, naughty boy,' adds Irene.

Impossible to pretend that I don't know them, that they've made a mistake. I'm just not quick enough off the mark. It's far too complicated to attempt.

They seat themselves. Beatriz approaches. I try not to say more than I need, although the damage is done.

They order in English. I order another coffee, in Spanish.

She walks away. I watch her shoulders become small, like those of a child.

The conversation develops. I try to resist the talk of mutual acquaintances but can't for long. Impossible to sit there and say nothing.

They talk loudly these women. They dominate any space they are in. It's their way. If Beatriz were hiding in the kitchen she would hear every word.

'So, Alfredo Martinez is dead.'

'Not before time.'

'*Irene!* Terrible!' Valentina snorts.

'Come on, but it's true. He was ancient. They absolutely *stuffed* him for the coffin. He'd lost a *lot* of weight.'

'And such a handsome man once. He really could have done with some work before such a public display.'

'*Mean* of you not to offer, Julio Ortiz. A gentleman like you.'

'I'm no longer able, as perhaps you know – my hands,' I say. 'And it's not yet *standard* practice to offer a facelift to a corpse.'

'You can do me any day,' Irene drawls. 'Dead or alive.'

'Me too!' Valentina adds.

'But what about your hands? Don't you try to tell me that they've lost their touch.'

'Irene.'

'Now, don't be coy. We all know who has the magician's fingers in BA!'

They laugh together. They are in fits at this smut.

I can't help it; I am chuckling too.

They leave ahead of me, with promises of drinks, very soon, from all of us.

I linger on in the café, not sure what it is that I am waiting for. Beatriz has left the bill on the table. There is no further need for her to appear. I know she will not.

I take out my wallet and rifle for notes. My hand is shaking, yet again, and I drop it on the floor.

I have to get down on my knees. I gather up the notes that have fallen, pick up my wallet and, overheated, sit back in my chair.

I am still clasping a handful of notes. I put them away, and leave the precise amount on the bill, no more, no less, in small change.

I walk away from my table and out of the door, without looking back. I feel profound melancholy. The door swings shut.

★

Pay attention. This is important.

She is not beautiful. Her face is not symmetrical. As a rule of thumb beauty requires symmetry and, as with so many people, the two sides of her face don't match.

Her left eye opens wider than her right –
when she is tired her right eye can look half closed.
In fact, there is a kind of heaviness to the right side
of her face, as if it were somehow more susceptible
– to what... gravity, grief?

Her lower lip is larger than her upper, and
there is a jaggedness to the outline of the upper
that is at odds with the whole. She has a dimple
that is stretching to a deep line on her right cheek.

A smoker. Indeed, we have smoked together.
It is a passion we share. I know, regardless, that she
has smoked for some years, from the traces of lines
on her upper lip; again, on the right.

Her left-hand side is something else. Her eye
is bright and alert, a sense of humour always close
at hand. She has green eyes, I may not have
mentioned. Whereas on the right the lines that
cluster around her eye add age and some sadness,
on the left they appear to bear witness to laughter,
joie de vivre.

She has a minimal cleft in her chin – almost
another dimple – which lends her face strength
overall.

When she smokes, she plants the cigarette
between her teeth, in the very centre, as she lights
it. Her first drag then is forthright, determined,
before the cigarette wanders off to the right and
hangs loosely, as if it might drop from her lips.

She has dark hair. It is of medium length, and
most often tied back.

She is moderately tall.

She is – to hazard a guess, taking into account

the puffiness beneath the eyes, the lines now visible on her forehead, the loss of youthful volume in her lips – in her late thirties.

She has a small waist. She has scarred hands.

About the Authors

Tahmina Anam is an anthropologist and novelist. Her debut novel, *A Golden Age*, was winner of the 2008 Commonwealth Writers Prize for Best First Book. In 2013, she was named one of Granta's Best Young British Novelists. She is a Contributing Opinion Writer for *The New York Times* and a judge for the 2016 Man Booker International Prize. Born in Dhaka, Bangladesh, she was educated at Mount Holyoke College and Harvard University and now lives in Hackney, East London.

Claire-Louise Bennett's debut collection of short stories, *Pond* was published in the UK by Fitzcarraldo in Autumn 2015. It has been translated into several languages including Spanish, Dutch, German and Norwegian, and is published in the US by Riverhead Books. It was recently shortlisted for the Dylan Thomas Prize. Claire-Louise's stories and essays have appeared in *The White Review, Guernica, The Irish Times, gorse*, and *Paper Visual Art Journal*, among others. This year she has produced art writing for Temple Bar Gallery & Studios,

Nottingham Contemporary, the Tate, and 126 Artist-Led Gallery.

Lavinia Greenlaw is a writer who lives in London. She studied seventeenth-century art and her interest in perception, optical technologies, landscape and questions of travel led to her being the first artist in residence at the Science Museum. She has published five collections of poetry, most recently *A Double Sorrow: Troilus and Criseyde* (Faber 2014). Her other works include two novels and the memoir, *The Importance of Music to Girls* (Faber 2007). *Audio Obscura*, her immersive soundwork for Artangel/Manchester International Festival won the 2011 Ted Hughes Award. Her first short film, *The Sea is an Edge and an Ending*, a study of the impact of dementia on our sense of time and place, drawing on Shakespeare's *The Tempest*, will premiere at the Estuary Festival in September 2016. She also writes about music, perception and art. Her commissions have included pieces on Joy Division for the *London Review of Books*, a total solar eclipse for *The New Yorker*, and a poem to mark the centenary of the Theory of Relativity for the Science Museum. Her work for radio includes documentaries about vision and light with subjects ranging from Arctic midsummer and midwinter to a year-long study of the solstices and equinoxes in Britain. She has also written and directed several radio dramas. Formerly Professor of Poetry at the University of East Anglia, she has been a Visiting Professor at King's College London and will be the

Samuel Fischer Guest Professor at the Freie Universität Berlin in Spring 2017.

Hilary Mantel grew up in the Peak District in Derbyshire and was educated at a Cheshire convent school, LSE and Sheffield University, graduating in law in 1973. She was subsequently a teacher and a social worker, living for nine years in Africa and the Middle East. She became a full-time writer in the mid 1980s, and is the author of eleven novels, two short story collections and a memoir, *Giving Up The Ghost*. She writes both historical and contemporary fiction and her settings range from a South African township under apartheid to Paris in the Revolution, from a city in twentieth century Saudi Arabia to rural Ireland in the eighteenth century.

Her novel *Wolf Hall* is about Thomas Cromwell, chief minister to Henry VIII. It won the 2009 Man Booker prize, the inaugural Walter Scott prize, and in the US won the National Book Critics Circle Award.

Her second Cromwell novel, *Bring Up The Bodies*, won the 2012 Man Booker Prize and the Costa 'Book of the year' Award. Both novels were adapted for television, and she worked with the adapter Mike Poulton on a stage version which was performed in Stratford on Avon, the West End and Broadway. She is a Governor of The Royal Shakespeare Company. In 2014 she published a book of short stories *The Assassination of Margaret Thatcher*. She is currently working on the final novel of the Thomas Cromwell trilogy *The Mirror & The Light*. She was appointed DBE in 2014. She lives with her husband in East Devon.

K J Orr was born in London. *Light Box*, her first collection of short stories, was published in February 2016. Her stories have appeared in publications including *Best British Short Stories 2015*, *Beta-Life,* the *Irish Times*, the *Dublin Review*, the *White Review* and the *Sunday Times Magazine*, and have been recognised by numerous awards including the BBC National Short Story Award and the Bridport Prize. She studied at St Andrews, UEA, and Chichester, and has published essays and reviews in *Poetry Review*, the *TLS* and *The Guardian*, among others.

About the Award

THE BBC NATIONAL SHORT STORY AWARD with BookTrust is one of the most prestigious prizes for a single short story and celebrates the best in home-grown short fiction. The ambition of the Award, which is now in its eleventh year, is to expand opportunities for British writers, readers and publishers of the short story. The winning author receives £15,000, the runner-up £3,000 and the three further shortlisted authors £500 each. All five shortlisted stories are broadcast on BBC Radio 4.

The previous winners are: Jonathan Buckley (2015), Lionel Shriver (2014), Sarah Hall (2013), Miroslav Penkov (in 2012, when the Award accepted international entries to commemorate the Olympics); D. W. Wilson (2011); David Constantine (2010); Kate Clanchy (2009); Clare Wigfall (2008); Julian Gough (2007) and James Lasdun (2006).

Award Partners:

BBC RADIO 4 is the world's single biggest commissioner of short stories. Short stories are broadcast every week attracting more than a million listeners.
www.bbc.co.uk/radio4

BookTrust is Britain's largest reading charity. It has a vision of a society where nobody misses out on the life-changing benefits that reading can bring. BookTrust is responsible for a number of successful national reading promotions, sponsored book prizes and creative reading projects aimed at encouraging readers to discover and enjoy books. www.booktrust.org.uk

More on: www.booktrust.org.uk/bbcnssa
Follow us on Twitter: @BookTrust #BBCNSSA